2037
The End
of Tolerance

Luke Mauerman

Mauerman, Luke
2037

First Edition
Library of Congress Control Number: 2019905201

ISBN 978-1-7330257-0-6 (paperback)

Published by
Beekman Place Editions
Desert Hot Springs, California

Cover/interior design
Mark E. Anderson

 AquaZebra™
Web, Book & Print Design
www.aquazebra.com

Printed in the United States of America

Chapter 1

The earthquake struck at 1:13 p.m. on May 19, 2022. Stephe Stafford, age fourteen, was at Mission High School in San Francisco in P.E. class when it hit. They were playing basketball in the gym. He'd just proudly blocked a pass—he didn't like sports much and spent most of his time avoiding the ball—when the floor started buckling amid a horrific roar.

Stephe, like everyone else, dropped where he stood to the floorboards. It was difficult to stand anyway. The slats buckled and cracked; a huge section tore apart and began to lift, several girls straddling it scrambled to get away from the fissure. It was finally four inches wide. The arc lights above swung madly, casting insane shadows and floods of light on the huddled students. The coveted basketball rolled past him, and Stephe had the strange desire, despite his fear, to grab it, to possess it. He grabbed on and held it to his stomach, in the fetal position, waiting for doom to strike. The earthquake seemed to go on forever.

The Mission High School gym managed to hold together. Many of the older sections of the school's walls didn't fare as well. Several caved in around the school.

The shaking eventually stopped and students slowly got back to their feet, with shoulders up, hugging each other and slapping each other on the back. "Man! That was scary shit!" "Are you okay?" "Is everyone okay?"

The gym instructor, Mr. Bogrand, blew his whistle and waved everyone out of the gym. "C'mon, outside. *Now!* Move it!"

The students fled out the side door and gathered on the sidewalk on Church Street, joined by students from all over the school. To the north, one wall had caved in, opening Mrs. Sylvester's history class to the street.

In the rapidly growing crowd, Stephe found his friend Ben. They hugged.

"Holy *shit!*" Ben yelled, pointing to the history room. "We were in there when the wall collapsed. I don't think anyone was hurt. We were damned lucky! We just climbed through the wall to the outside."

The throng of students grew ever larger, spilling out onto Church Street, nosing into their phones, sharing their stories, telling their tales and making sure their friends were all right.

"I was in the gym," Stephe said. "It held together but the floor was shattered."

Ben had his iPhone out. "No signal," he said.

After twenty minutes with no information or instruction from any of the teachers, Stephe told Ben he was going to walk home to check on his house.

"Good idea," said Ben. "I might as well go too; I think school is effectively out for the day."

Stephe, still in his gym clothes, and Ben, eyes glued to his dead phone, walked down Church Street together, turned right, and headed up 18th.

The neighborhood was in tatters. Beautiful wooden Victorians stood visibly off plumb. Some houses had crumbled, especially the 1960s buildings. Cars were stopped. Traffic on 18th Street quickly snarled as debris fell and people couldn't get through.

Ben and Stephe parted at Sanchez Street. Stephe continued

up the tight, steep hill to 472 Liberty Street, to the dark blue house in which he'd grown up. He was relieved to see it still standing. He realized he didn't have his keys; they were still in his locker at school, along with his iPhone. As he surveyed the outside of the house—which looked normal as far as he could tell—he found a broken window at the garage. He poked out the shards with his sneakers to gain access, his heart pounding in fear. What would he find inside?

He got inside and jumped down to the floor. He was in the tiny garage, crowded by the family Prius. It looked mostly normal but items were knocked off the shelves over the washer and dryer, a jug of Tide oozing onto the floor. He picked it up. Once he was up the basement stairs, he discovered the door to the kitchen was stuck, but it finally opened when he gave it a heavy shove. Pots were off the shelves and dishes were broken; a crack was creeping across the ceiling plaster and dust was everywhere. He ran up to his room to find a mess—it was always messy—but his bed had slid out from the wall and there was a crack in the ceiling and chunks of plaster were down. His black and white tuxedo cat, Lilo, was standing on his bed looking rattled. Stephe petted her; she dove her head into his leg as he sat down and she purred tentatively. Yet her tail still twitched and she quickly looked back up to nervously eye the room.

Moana, the other Siamese cat, was nowhere to be seen.

He surveyed the large house, going room to room, checking for damage. His brother Jack's room, right across the hall from his own, looked fine. Jack was away at school in Chicago. There were two other bedrooms used as offices and storage on the second story, and his parent's room on the top floor. He found the same in every room; cracks in walls and items tossed about. He found Moana in his parent's room asleep on the bed in a sea of dust.

From his parent's bedroom at the peak of the house Stephe could gaze out to a view of the city. What he saw was shocking: A thick haze hung in the distance over everything, several buildings were down, and the Castro Theatre sign was hanging at a crazy angle. The skyscrapers downtown looked solid and resolute, but something was just "off"—he couldn't put his finger on it. Most alarming were the fires burning across town: furious billows of black smoke at several areas in the Mission District to his right and another behind Buena Vista Park. Haight Ashbury was on fire. Sirens blared in the distance. To the left, over Twin Peaks, the fog oozed over the hill as if nothing happened.

His parents were at work and he was alone with no phone—not that the cell service would probably be working. With nothing to do and the house more or less okay, he went back to his room and began cleaning it up.

Stephe realized he was hungry. It was only when he opened the microwave for some Hot Pockets from the freezer that he realized the power was out. Even so, he went to the TV in the living room and grabbed the remote. He was surprised that he hadn't guessed the TV would be of no use.

Since school was nearby, he wanted to go back and get his phone in case his parents tried to call and could get through. He changed out of his gym clothes, gave Lilo another scritch, and headed back down the hill.

By this time, the crowd of students surrounding the school had thinned out. He wondered how he was going to manage getting into the locker room undetected; people and staff wandered aimlessly around and Burt, the security guard, was waving people away. When Burt was turned, Stephe ducked under some yellow police tape and snuck back into the empty gym. The floor was in wooden tatters and the arc lamps were still swaying slightly. How long had it been? Forty-five minutes?

He got to the deserted changing room, spun the dial on his lock, and grabbed his phone and keys from the pocket of his jeans. He was dying to check his phone, but decided it was best to get out of there first, lest he got caught.

Once back on Church Street and safely past Burt, once again just a citizen on the sidewalk, he opened his phone. No messages. He dialed his mom. All he got was a fast busy signal. He tried Facebook, CNN, *SF Chronicle*, KTVU. Nothing. The pages wouldn't draw.

He sent a text to his mom, but it wouldn't deliver; it just sat there with half a bar across the screen. Finally the screen said "Failed To Send" in red. He hit re-send several times but only got the same error message.

Stephe's parents both worked in Millennium Tower, a 58-story building constructed in 2009. Originally designed to be luxury condominiums, the tower famously began sinking and tilting to one side shortly after it was built. People sued and moved out. Windows kept popping from the stresses on the building. But as with all things financial, instead of tearing it down, some foundation modifications were made to supposedly stop it from sagging any further and they went on to re-lease it as commercial office space—much more profitable. So that's where his parents both worked—Stephen Stafford as a graphics designer on the 10th floor and Diane Stafford an attorney on the 46th.

Stephe was aching to know if his parents were okay. With no phones he would just have to wait until they managed to get home.

People were still standing in idle groups talking outside the school but he didn't see anyone he knew. He decided to head back up 18th Street to Starbucks, dodging piles of debris and a few cars parked on the sidewalk. The plate glass windows of Starbucks were shattered. The lights were out and the darkened interior devoid of people. But people were standing around on the sidewalk, some still with coffee in their hands, gathered into small groups. Stephe saw his neighbor and fellow student Mark Benson and ran over to him.

"Hey!"

"Hey," Mark answered, and they gave each other a quick hug. "How about this shit! Have you been home? Is everything okay?"

"Yeah," Stephe replied, "my house is okay. Things got knocked around and there's lots of cracks. But the cats are okay. I just can't reach my parents." He waved his phone around helplessly.

"Same here. The power's out so I decided to come down here. I guess the Muni underground is closed. There's fires everywhere. Some big buildings downtown collapsed completely."

The news struck Stephe. "No shit? My parents work in Millennium Tower, the one that was already sinking."

"Yeah, I heard that. I did get a text from my mom. She's in Daly City trying to drive home. She doesn't know how long it'll take. Could be hours."

It felt good to Stephe to be able to speak to someone— anyone—even Mark Benson, with whom he rarely talked in school.

"I was in math class," Mark continued. "Mrs. Crosby was freaking out, arms waving, yelling at everyone to get under their desks. I was under mine in half a second. It was funny at first, then it got way too real. I think we were all scared shitless by the end."

"I was playing basketball in the gym. Nowhere to hide," Stephe replied.

Stephe decided to go back home. He didn't like tales of buildings collapsing. Almost as an afterthought he took a few half-hearted pictures of the broken Starbucks and a few shattered homes on his way back up the hill to Liberty Street.

Thank God for bedrock. None of the houses on his street seemed to have been affected.

The emptiness of the house was eerie. The air was close. It was quiet—too quiet; not even the hum of the refrigerator in the background. The only noise was a fly, buzzing around, butting against the window above the kitchen sink.

He pondered how long it might take to hear from his parents. Millennium Tower was at First and Mission Streets, so, with the subway out of service, it would be a good two-hour walk home.

He had a bowl of cereal; when he went to rinse out the bowl, he found the water was out, too.

No phones, no lights, no water. He took stock of the darkened fridge; leftovers would get him by for a while. The Arrowhead water cooler in the corner was still full of drinking water.

Just then someone knocked on the front door. It was Helga, his next door neighbor.

"I just wanted to make sure everything was okay," she said.

"Everything seems fine, thanks. A couple of cracks and broken dishes. I can't get ahold of my parents, though. It'll take them hours to walk home."

"Well, I'm sure they'll get here as soon as they can," she said reassuringly. "Do you have enough food?"

"Yeah, I've got some," he replied. "I can defrost stuff from the freezer and cook it on the gas grill I suppose."

"Well, if you need anything, or just want to come over, please let us know. Robert left his car at work and is walking home. He should be here in an hour or so," she said. "In fact, why don't you plan on coming over for dinner at six? We'll just have chicken and coleslaw, but you're welcome to come eat with us if your parents aren't back yet."

"Thanks! I will." He realized that sitting alone in a broken house with two cats and a buzzing fly was going to get on his nerves. "I'm going over to Noe Street to check on my best friend, Ben."

"Okay, well, be safe out there! Watch for downed power lines. Have your parents stop by when they get home," she said from the bottom step.

Stephe was glad for his idea to go to Ben's house. He hated being alone. It was just coming on 3:30. He left a note for his parents, locked the door, and set out along the hill. The view was startling: The fires had spread. Huge swaths of the Mission were burning, as was the Haight. A lot of old wooden buildings, and if there was no water—he shuddered at the thought, hoping his house would be safe.

He got to Ben's house at Nineteenth and Noe Streets in just a few minutes. The houses along the hill all looked okay, again because of the bedrock beneath them. He could see down to 18th Street, and the cars still jammed up.

Ben answered the door. "Glad to see you!'

"You too! Is everything all right?

"Come in and check it out! Our dining room ceiling popped down and the fridge slid two feet!"

Stephe followed him inside and saw the lath and plaster down upon the dining room table and scattered on the floor.

"My mom's gonna *shit* when she sees this," laughed Ben. "I'm not even allowed in the dining room because she thinks I'll mess it up. Hah!"

They went up to his room and sat on the bed.

"My phone's not working, is yours?"

"Naw. It's still toast," Ben answered. "We have a landline and I tried to call my mom in Redwood City, but it's dead as a doornail."

"This sucks!" Stephe said.

"Yeah. If I'm lucky I won't hear from her any time soon." Ben's mom was known to be a little difficult—a single mom who was always yelling about something.

"There's no power, no water, no Internet, no TV. I wish we could get news of how big this thing is," Stephe said.

"It was probably the Hayward Fault—that's the one they always said would bring the next Big One. I bet Oakland is on its *ass* right now!"

As they sat on the bed a sizable aftershock struck; everything jiggled and jounced and they could hear a muted roar. It startled them both. But it was over quickly, and nothing like the main event. Ben's dog, Lucy, a bichon, came tearing into the room and jumped on the bed next to Ben.

They sat and talked, about the quake, about the fires. They decided to snag some popsicles from the freezer. As Ben had said, the stainless side-by-side fridge had slid to the length of its cord, still plugged in to the dead outlet. Stephe helped Ben push it back to where it belonged.

They sat in the living room and played Zombie on their phones via Bluetooth for a while. Then when Ben said he didn't want his battery to get too low, they stopped.

"Jesus," said Ben. "It's so fucking quiet and boring. There's nothing to do!"

"I know," Stephe replied. "I don't want to just sit alone in my house, but I want to be there when my parents get home. I should go."

"Yeah. I get it. Send me a text when they get home." He checked himself and rolled his eyes. "Sorry. Send a smoke signal."

"Too much smoke already. I'll beat it out on my drum." Ben smiled and gave him a chuck on the arm. "See you—only not at school, I think that ship has sailed."

"I'll come by tomorrow," Stephe promised.

"'Okay. Good luck!" Ben said in parting.

Stephe headed back over to the house. The fires in the Mission were worse. It was a black wall of smoke about a mile-and-a-half away, and flames could be seen, licking upward in several locations.

Back home his note was still by the door. No word from his parents. So he fed the cats. Lilo had calmed down and Moana was as unrattled as ever.

Failing anything to do he got into bed with a book, *No Time Like Tomorrow,* his favorite 1960's novel about a teen who travels through time. He read until the fog rolled in, making the light dim and useless. It was about time to go next door for dinner.

He wrote a new note to his parents, telling them where he'd be.

Robert Adams was home and answered the door, giving Stephe a quick hug.

"How about this, huh?" he asked, leading Stephe into the house. "My office was in a shambles and the computers were out so we called it a day. I'm glad I work at UCSF on Parnassas. It was only about an hour's walk home. But you don't want to be in the Haight right now. The fires are out of control. I'm pretty worried . . ."

"Hi, Stephe," Helga called from the kitchen door. "I just managed to straighten the place back up. Did you feel the aftershock?"

"Yeah," he replied. "It was a little . . . uncomfortable."

"Yes, I think we've had enough for one day," Robert said.

"Well, let's eat!" Helga waved her hand dramatically and Stephe saw the kitchen table well set with a yellow tablecloth, flowers and several lit candles. A bottle of red wine, a plate of fried chicken and a dish of coleslaw sat waiting, just as advertised.

"You want a Coke?" Helga asked.

"Yes, please," Stephe answered, seating himself at the table at the place set without a wine glass.

Helga produced a can from the dark refrigerator. "Sorry, no ice. We're saving it for unforseeables. Plus, it's melting anyway."

"No problem. Thank you!" The Coke was just a little warmer than fridge temperature but tasted cool and sweet and fizzy, just the same.

Helga dished up a chicken breast, wing and leg for the three of them and passed the dish of coleslaw around. Stephe took a modest portion.

They ate in silence. Rob and Helga drank heavily from the wine.

Feeling the need to converse, Stephe described the earthquake from his perspective in the gym . . . how he grabbed the basketball as the only thing to hold onto.

Robert said he was in a meeting and the ceiling tiles all fell loose from their metal slats and rained down upon them, but being so light, they didn't hurt anybody. Then the power was out.

"They're saying it was the Hayward Fault," Robert mused. "BART's shut down, the Muni underground is out, and lots of buildings collapsed all over. They say there's no water to fight the fires."

"I was on eBay," Helga said, "in my office upstairs when it hit; I was just about to bid on a vase when the computer blew out. My chair rolled halfway across the wooden floor with me still in it! I think I have most of this stuff cleaned up, but we'll have to get all the cracks looked at. Lath and plaster don't bend in an earthquake, they just break. Part of the pitfalls of an older house, I guess."

Stephe nodded appreciatively, "Mm-hmm." He was glad to be there, but a queasiness had been growing all day in the pit of his stomach. When would his parents get home? They had plenty of time to walk home by now.

It was there at the table with Robert and Helga that genuine fear began to grip him. He had to force himself to finish the fried chicken and wash it down with the last of the Coke from the can.

"Would you like more?" Helga asked. "There's plenty."

"No, thank you," Stephe replied. "This was great! Thanks!"

"Sure, Stephe. You're welcome. Stay as long as you like; we can play board games," she offered.

Stephe was appreciative but the uneasiness growing in his belly had him wishing he were back home. Even if it meant being alone.

He took his leave of the Adams's as graciously as he could, remembering to thank them as his mother, Diane, had always taught him to do.

He went up to his parent's room and sat on the dusty bed. He gazed at the cracks in the gabled ceiling above their bed, which was made up every morning by his mom before she went to work.

His parents, Stephen and Diane, were married in 2002 in Colorado; they had Jack right away and Stephe five years later. They moved to San Francisco in 2007. Jack was in college at Northwestern University, probably wondering what was going on back home. He'd have TV and Internet—in a way, Jack knew much more than Stephe did.

Sitting on the bed he tried his phone again. It had a single bar; he re-sent the text to his mom and this time it went through! He called her phone and it rang! A raspy, scratchy connection but it rang and rang until he heard, "Hello, you've reached Diane Stafford, I'm unavailable right now. Please leave me a message." And then the T-Mobile computer voice said, "Please leave your message. When you have finished recording, you may hang up, or press Pound for more options." *Beep.*

Stephe immediately began speaking into his phone: "Mom! It's me. I'm home, everything's okay, the house is fine. Where are you? Please call me back when you can! I'm okay but the power's out. Call me?" He hesitated, but ended with "I love you." Then he paused before hitting the red END button. But he did so, ending the call.

So that was that.

He did the same to his father's phone number, got voice-mail, left a message.

Next he tried to call Jack in Chicago. Jack picked up on the first ring: "Stephe! Are you okay?"

"Yeah, I'm fine . . ."

"How are Mom and Dad? How's the house?"

Stephe's voice choked a little. Jack hadn't heard from them either.

"The house is fine, the power and water are out—but I haven't heard from Mom and Dad. They should be home by now . . ."

He could hear Jack exhale on the phone.

"Shit. A few skyscrapers in San Francisco have collapsed. It's all over the news. The damage is pretty incredible."

"Jack, what are we going to do if we don't hear anything?" Stephe's voice was cracking at this point, the sick feeling in his belly becoming a sharp pain and his heart pounding.

"Don't worry, little brother, I'm sure they're fine."

"I just don't know what to do; there's no one to ask." The strain of the day was starting to break through. Stephe was sounding hysterical. "Why won't they come home?"

"Keep calm, Stephe. They'll be there. The streets are blocked and it'll take them hours to get through. They probably stopped by Absinthe to get roaring drunk on their way home. You know how Dad gets."

That much was true. Stephen Stafford was quite the drinker. Always a happy, beneficent drunk, he wouldn't let a calamity go by without raising a glass.

Stephe forced himself to be calm to ask his brother, "Tell me what you know. We have no information here."

Jack began, "It was an 8.8 on the Hayward Fault, centered in Morgan Hill. Heavy damage and fires in the East Bay. Downtown Oakland is a mess. Berkeley, San Leandro, Dublin, Castro Valley—there's fires and collapsed buildings everywhere. The bridges are closed, BART's shut down, traffic in the streets is so bad that nobody can get through. Fires in the Mission District and Haight Ashbury are burning out of control. All the buildings are made of wood, and without water there's nothing to stop them. CPMC Pacific Hospital had to be evacuated; they're using the synagogue next door for triage. The news just keeps showing drone footage of the fires and collapsed buildings."

"What about Millennium Tower? That's where Mom and Dad both work and that building had been sinking ever since it was built . . ." Stephe trailed off.

"Well, I don't know, little brother. I just don't know," Jack replied. "They say some skyscrapers buckled, and we can see in the drone footage big piles of rubble various places downtown and South of Market. You know how the buildings all look alike down there."

"Yeah," Stephe responded reluctantly.

"So they're getting help from wherever they can. Fire crews are coming up from San Jose, Santa Rosa, and in from Sacramento just as fast as they can."

"What should I do?" Stephe asked.

"Well, you just gotta hang tight," Jack responded, trying to encourage his younger sibling. "Do you have food and water?"

"Yeah," Stephe replied.

"I guess just stay home unless the fires get too close to the Castro, then you'll have to evacuate." Jack thought for a minute, then asked, "Do you have a backpack?"

"Yes."

"Get ready to bug out if the Mission Fires come your way," Jack told him. "I'm sure they'll tell everyone to evacuate if it becomes necessary, but the fires are still a mile off."

"I will," Stephe assured him. "I'll get ready."

"Good boy. And don't worry about Mom and Dad I'm sure they're—"

Beep beep beep.

The call went dead. The one precious bar of cell reception on his screen had winked out and gone blank.

Millennium Tower! Stephe sat on his parent's bed. It was getting dark and gray and foggy. He just sat. Both cats came and jumped on the bed, but still he sat.

He finally went back down to his room and packed his backpack with various things he thought he might need: a flashlight, a change of clothes, his toothbrush, and phone chargers. He was glad for something proactive to do. But once that was over he got into bed. He began to lose it. He started crying into his pillow—great, hacking sobs—for quite a while. Eventually it passed. He blew his nose twice and curled up with his pillow in the fetal position and tensely waited.

Fire scared him. It always had. But he forced himself to think logically: The ever-present wind in San Francisco blew from the ocean in the west toward the bay in the east. That meant the fires wouldn't come his way unless the wind shifted. And it never did.

His parents were another matter. He would try to sleep, only to jerk awake again, heart pounding, sick to his stomach. Finally, after what seemed like hours, he drifted off to sleep.

Chapter 2

His parents never came home. Millennium Tower was one of four skyscrapers that collapsed on that day. Thousands of lives were lost. As with the terrorist attacks of September 11, 2001, most remains could never be positively identified.

Stephe awoke the next morning in dread to a still-too-quiet house. No parents. He quickly ran upstairs to see how far away the fires were. They were still a long way off and looked partially under control.

He fixed himself some more cereal, fed the cats, and struck out with his backpack. He was going to Millennium Tower to see for himself what the situation was. He had remembered his father's hi-viz vest stored in the basement from his Neighborhood Emergency Response Training, and added it to his backpack.

The Red Cross had set up a tent at Harvey Milk Plaza. Stephe went there first and dully recited his personal information which was recorded on a laptop: Parents missing, Stephen and Diane Stafford, Millennium Tower. After that he just started walking in the direction of downtown. He had nowhere else to go.

Market Street was eerily quiet. Everything was closed. There was broken glass everywhere. Some of the debris had already been shunted aside; traffic was moving again but the antique street cars were stopped at various places, the power lines down.

He walked and walked. Down the hill past Safeway which was open and had some lights on; the place was mobbed, with people directing traffic in and out of the packed parking lot.

It was a foggy, overcast day. Nevertheless, he worked up a sweat walking to Mission and Fremont Streets. It took him an hour and a half, only to be blocked at Market and First. Yellow tape and firetrucks and heavy moving equipment formed a barrier that ran for several blocks in every direction. Still, he wasn't going to be deterred. He pulled the hi-viz vest out of his back-pack, donned it, and ducked the tape.

He got as far as Fremont and Market before being chased out by a cop; at only fourteen years of age, the hi-viz was only going to get him so far in the confusion. But what he saw between the buildings filled his heart with dread. Mission Street, one block down, was nothing but a pile of rubble some nine stories tall. It was in complete ruin. The cop brusquely shoved Stephe back toward the tape amid threats of arrest. Stephe didn't try to argue; he saw what he came to see.

Millennium Tower was no more.

He walked home, slowly, aimlessly. Tears blurred his vision and he felt like throwing up. He got as far as Bank of America at Van Ness by the time he just melted down onto the sidewalk and cried. It felt impossible that his parents could be alive, yet impossible they were dead. There were no answers to be had, and he filled with rage at the unfairness of it all. He sat sobbing for an immeasurable time.

Finally, he could cry no more and his butt hurt and he smelled dry piss on the concrete, so he got back up and started walking again. Back up Market Street, occasionally hacking great sobs. He headed slowly for home and suddenly hated that house. He didn't want to go back there by himself.

When had he last seen them? What had they last said to each other? What did they even look like? He pictured his mother and father when he saw them yesterday morning, rushing out the door to commute together, stainless steel coffee mugs in hand; walking to the F-Market line as they did every morning. Or did they take the Muni Underground? His dad preferred the street cars; his mom said they took too long, that the Underground was faster. "Too crowded," his father would always say.

Finally he got home, detesting the house, yet still with a dim hope his parents would be there.

Only the cats greeted him—and half-heartedly.

Stephe ran upstairs to his room and flung himself on his bed and let it all loose again, wracked with sobs so deep he could hardly breathe. He didn't want to breathe. Every inhale was a confirmation of this new truth in which he found himself trapped. He cried himself to sleep.

By the time he woke up it was about 2:00 in the afternoon, the day after the earthquake. He was hungry, even though he didn't feel as though he deserved to eat. He thought about getting cold cuts and cheese out of the darkened refrigerator when someone turned the old key, ringing the doorbell. It was Helga from next door.

"Any word, honey?"

Stephe shook his head "no" and said, "I just walked back from Millennium Tower. It's gone."

Helga rushed to him and locked him in a great hug. "I'm so sorry, Stephe . . . I'm so sorry."

He didn't cry. But he held onto his neighbor, trembling.

"Come next door," she insisted.

He followed, not even bothering to close the front door. Robert was there, and, seeing the look on his wife's face grabbed Stephe's hand with both of his and gave it a firm shake. "I'm sorry, Stephe."

He choked on his mumbled "Thanks."

"We're just having sandwiches," Robert said, clearing his throat. "Join us."

"Thanks." Stephe mumbled again.

They ate on paper plates in the living room—chicken sandwiches, potato chips and warm Cokes.

"We have a spare room," Helga began. "We were going to open it up for refugees—thousands of homeless people are in the city who need places to go. But why don't you take it instead, Stephe? Stay with us. As long as you need. You can't stay alone in that great big empty house."

Stephe had a mouthful of potato chips and could only nod. He washed it down with some Coke before answering, grateful for the second or two to let his thoughts scurry through his head. He liked the idea. The loneliness at home was overpowering.

"I think I'd like that," he was finally able to answer.

Suddenly Robert's cellphone rang in his pocket. It was such a simple, everyday sound, but Stephe's belly flooded at relief at such a soothing normal thing as a phone call. Suddenly, Stephe felt his own phone buzz madly, too.

"It's Brian," Robert said and answered the phone.

"Brian! We're fine, thanks!" he said. "How's Trish? The kids?" He listened. "Good! Oh, so glad to hear. Yeah, the power's still out. We're looking after our neighbor, Stephe, here. . . . Good to hear your voice, too."

Their conversation continued and Stephe quickly put down his paper plate and fished his own phone out of his pocket. Full bars! Seven text messages bleeped in—none from his parents—but two from Jack, three from Ben, and two from Emergency Alert Services talking about the earthquake and possible evacuation warnings.

Diane had her phone out too, scrolling through messages.

Robert finished up his phone call. "That was Brian," he said again, unnecessarily. "They're fine."

"I have a text from Lisa," Diane offered. "She's good. And a bunch from Emergency Alert Services. Well, those are pretty useless."

"Me too," said Robert, studying his phone.

"This calls for a mini-celebration," Helga declared. "I'm going to have a warm beer and start calling and texting people."

Stephe didn't have much power left on his phone. The texts from Jack were from before their short phone call last night, asking how he was. Ben's texts were usual Ben stuff, complaining about being bored and about his mom who walked in at 8:00 last night.

Plates and sandwiches—and politeness—forgotten, both Robert and Helga were immediately on their phones calling various people. Stephe thought, with a lump in his throat, about calling his parents again, but he just couldn't. It wouldn't do any good. He couldn't bear the thought of hearing their voices on their voicemails. He sat on the sofa and called Jack back. Once again, he picked up on the first ring.

"Stephe! How's it going? Have you heard from Mom and Dad?"

"Jack," Stephe began, yet felt another sob forming in his throat. "Millennium Tower's gone. I just got back from there..."

Jack sighed. "Yes. It was on the news last night. It's completely gone. Shit. I just kept hoping they were wrong."

"They're gone, Jack." Stephe gave in to crying again. "They're gone."

Jack was crying, too. "I kept trying to hope, y'know? Maybe they weren't there when it hit. Maybe they were at lunch. Maybe they had the wrong building down."

They continued to speak, but words weren't enough. Stephe finally said, "I can't believe they're gone. I don't know what to do. Robert and Helga have asked me to come stay with them and I think I will."

"I'm coming out there as soon as I can," Jack declared. "As soon as I can get a flight out of Chicago, I'll be there. I'm hoping for tomorrow."

"That would be great. I need to see you," Stephe replied.

"You will. That's a promise. We'll figure everything out when I get there. Just sit tight with the Adams's and you'll be okay. Stephe? I don't know how, but it's going to be okay, all right? I'm going to be home for the whole summer so we'll be together."

"All right."

"Hopefully, I'll see you tomorrow."

"Okay," Stephe replied.

"Take care, little brother. Try to hang in there. I love you," Jack said assuringly.

"I love you, too," Stephe responded.

"Goodbye," Jack said.

"G'bye," Stephe said.

And they hung up.

Stephe stayed the night at the Adams's in a small bed in a bright yellow-painted sewing room. Frilly lace everything and lots of cute bears and throw pillows. He grabbed onto a teddy bear and held it all night. Sleep wouldn't come for many hours as he kept reliving the horror of that smashed building with his parents inside.

The next day, Day Three, as promised, Jack showed up. He ran to Stephe and gave him a giant bear hug.

All the times when they were growing up and refused to get along melted in that hug. The two brothers knew that all they had left in the world was each other.

Jack came over to the Adams's and the four of them sat on the living room couches, making small talk and hemming and hawing. It was difficult to know what to talk about.

"I had a long talk with Margery," Jack finally said. Margery was their aunt, their mother's sister, living in Fort Collins, Colorado. "She might wind up coming out here to stay with us."

This was good news and bad news. All along Stephe had been wondering about the house. Would they even be able to keep it? He thought he was sure his parents had paid it off a few years ago, but he, as a fourteen year old, wouldn't be allowed to live in it alone. Jack was nineteen—would that be old enough? What about after the summer was over and Jack went back to school? Margery added a whole new element of safety, a fifty-something woman would definitely be old enough. But Margery was a joyless person. A nurse, a confirmed bachelorette, always terse and impatient.

"The house is paid off," Jack said, "so there's no reason we can't continue to stay there forever." He patted Stephe on the knee. "With Margery here, then, there's no need to worry about leaving. I probably won't go back to Northwestern this fall; I'm just going to wait and see how I feel when the time comes. I'd have always preferred to be at Stanford; I might as well re-apply."

With Jack home, Stephe thanked the Adams's for their hospitality and shuttled his few belongings back to his own bedroom at 472 Liberty Street. He left the teddy bear where he found it, hoping his tear stains wouldn't show.

He and Jack took turns sweeping up plaster in various rooms, getting the house back into passable condition. Many cracks remained in the walls and ceilings, full chunks of plaster were down throughout the house leaving lath visible underneath.

The fires were put out by the end of Day Two. The Mission fire got knocked down first. Miles of fire hoses were run from the Bay; it took precious hours to set up an intricate network of hoses and fire boats to get the Mission fire under control. The Mission and South of Market burned from Valencia to 5th Street; from Howard Street to 20th.

The Haight-Ashbury fire was another matter altogether— too far from any source of water to use fireboats. They had to rely on air drops; a steady roar of jets and propeller planes buzzed the city for two days, dropping water and red flame retardant. People fled in all directions; thousands of homes were destroyed, many ornate Victorians—including the famous Painted Ladies at Alamo Square. Precious homes that had survived urban renewal of the 1960s and the hippies of the '70s were lost. The University of San Francisco went up in flames, as did University of California Parnassus Hospital. Robert Adams's car was burned in the parking garage.

On Day Four the power came back on. Every cell phone was dead by then. Never had so many chargers been plugged in at one time; it nearly blew the power grid back out.

On Day Six Margery Johnson arrived from Colorado.

With tense hugs, Jack and Stephe greeted her at the house. Margery was a glum, negative person. Born in 1965, short, greying hair a thin nose, and a generally grim expression on her face were her usual traits. She never wore make-up. Terse, but with a bit of a sense of humor—very dry—sometimes you'd hear her let loose with a witticism or a bon mot... but not often. Politically conservative, any time talk of "big government" came up, she'd cluck her tongue and stammer "Oh Lord!" She pursed her face a lot; sneered a lot.

She made no speeches about "how things are going to go" or what kind of ship she was "going to run." Instead of taking Stephe and Jack's parent's room as her own she opted for the spare bedroom down the hall on the second floor. "Too many stairs. Gad." She arrived with only two suitcases.

Stephen and Diane Stafford were declared officially dead by the City on Day Fifteen. Identifying remains at the site of Millennium Tower was virtually impossible, and the rubble was only partially cleared by then. But badge scans showed they were both in Millennium Tower at the time of the earthquake.

A man and woman in suits with iPads came to the door to serve official notification, and to see that Stephe, a fourteen-year-old orphan, was all right. Finding both Jack and Margery in residence seemed to satisfy their curiosity, but Margery needed to be officially listed as guardian. They gave instructions on how to accomplish that. And then they left; leaving Stephe in tears and Jack stoically fighting to keep from crying.

A grand memorial service took place the very next day, on Day Sixteen. Everyone crowded into AT&T Park—which had suffered some damage that was quickly repaired. The stadium was packed; crowds lined up outside and into the streets. Jack, Stephe and Margery had seats in the third tier, and cried their way through speeches by Reverend Cecil Williams of Glide Memorial Church—critically damaged in the quake—and Mayor Mark Leno and Governor Gavin Newsom.

Thirty-six thousand people died in the Hayward Quake of 2022. It was by far the greatest loss of life on American soil since the Civil War.

Twenty-two thousand people died in San Francisco proper, mostly from the collapse of Millennium Tower and three other large buildings South of Market. The East Bay was in tatters. Virtually every pane of glass popped and shattered, injuring tens of thousands. Oakland was in ruins, the 580 interchange in Castro Valley had come down in the temblor. Freeways toppled, houses collapsed, apartment buildings pancaked and office buildings caved in. The cities of San Leandro, Alameda, Berkeley, Fruitvale, Union City, San Ramon, Dublin, Livermore . . . the damage was everywhere.

No lives were untouched; everyone lost somebody that day on May 19, 2022.

BART was restored in six weeks; the Bay Bridge in eight. Life slowly returned to normal. It was a long summer. Gradually the city began to clear rubble and start rebuilding.

But everyone was in mourning.

Grieving takes many forms. For Stephe it was a gradual, painful burn in his belly. Not knowing was the worst part—he found he was still holding on to the desperate wish that it was all a mistake, that his parents would be found. Then he would catch himself, berate himself for such stupid hope. Eating was difficult.

Margery got a nursing job at Davies Hospital just up the street. Being junior staff at her new hospital meant she had to work nights. Stephe and Jack rarely saw her. But they expressed their thanks to her many times. She was making a huge sacrifice, upsetting her life in Colorado to come take care of them.

Stephe and Jack spent a lot of time together that summer, their old rivalries and arguments forgotten. Margery wasn't much for emotional support.

"You doing okay?" Stephe asked Jack one night in July.

"Yeah," Jack replied, putting down a book and leaning back in his chair, rubbing his eyes. "I still can't sleep at night. Sometimes I still can't eat—I don't *want* to eat. I can't believe Mom and Dad are gone."

"Me too. It hurts so bad."

"I can't help but think about it; how horrible it must've been for them. I like to pretend it was fast and they didn't suffer."

"How long do you think it took? How long were they afraid and alive and in pain? I picture them trapped and smashed and still alive." Stephe was looking at the floor, tears in his eyes.

"Don't go there, Stephe," Jack was firm. "It doesn't do any good."

"I know, but I can't help it. It's such a horrible way to die."

"It was quick. They probably didn't even know what happened."

Grief, after the initial shock of the loss, came in waves. Stephe would be minding his own business, getting on with his strange new half-life when, out of nowhere, tears would come, along with a queasy feeling in his belly. It was a physical pain sometimes.

The shock and grief stood with him always. He tried to remember everything about his parents, the good and the bad.

He used to rile his father, who was strict about his tools and chores around the house. They'd fight since Stephe never did his chores, or when he did, he didn't do them to his father's expectations. Stephen Senior was a graphic designer—a good one—born and raised in Colorado. He'd had blond, wavy hair and brown eyes, and he loved to fix up the house and putter around. He played golf a lot, and one time, when he caught Stephe whacking at rocks with his favorite nine-iron, had given his son quite a spanking. They had a canoe that they'd often take out on the Bay when the weather was nice.

Diane had been a brunette with blue eyes, and she was a very intelligent woman. She was a defense lawyer, specializing in asbestos cases. She was the more absent of the two parents, passing her bar exam when Stephe was only two—an heroic feat with a couple of small children at home. She was kind and warm, but she was always working. Thus, Stephen Senior served as father and mother to Stephe and Jack. He was definitely the more laid back of the two, the kind of dad you could go to with your problems and it would be okay. As long as you didn't use his nine-iron to hit rocks.

Stephe would weep, thinking of the things they did as a family; the trip to Washington, DC, in 2016 when Stephe was eight and Jack was thirteen; numerous camping trips, once to Yosemite. Diane brought her laptop on that trip, and plowed through work half the time they were there, charging it in the Prius.

You assume your parents are always going to be there; you never imagine they'll be smashed between blocks of concrete in their offices.

Stephen and Diane had been excited when they found out they'd be working in the same building. They commuted together in the morning, but Diane usually had to work late, while Stephen never did. He never seemed to bring his work home with him; Diane always did.

Stephe remembered his father trying to teach him the facts of life. He didn't know what a condom was and he once heard Jack say something about it and he asked, "What's a condom?" His dad showed him the package and opened one up and Stephe was mortified. He couldn't look his father in the eye for days afterward. He just stared at the carpet in humiliation.

Stephe and Jack loved each other as brothers do, but they used to fight endlessly. Stephe was never bright enough to compete with Jack; being five years older, Jack was always far ahead of Stephe and very competitive. Jack was a jock, while Stephe had an aversion to sports. Stephe was passive, very non-competitive, so his big brother would always with-hold things from him, ignoring him for no reason. Stephe always felt like he wasn't good enough for Jack; that he was the annoying younger brother, always crying.

But they needed each other now. Stephe was thankful every day that Jack was there.

The summer of 2022 wore on; construction was a constant backdrop everywhere, the city changing around them on a daily basis. It was dizzying.

Margery decided that, with two other bedrooms in the house, they would take in some refugees from the earthquake. Stephe liked the idea. It would do him some good to have other people around. Margery didn't count much as company, and Stephe hadn't seen much of his friend Ben that summer.

They took in four refugees from the fires: Pedro and Inez Guttierez from the Mission District, and Bob and Frank

Enwright—a gay couple from the Haight with an annoying Schnauzer named Coal. Lilo and Moana were quite put out, but everyone settled in to living in such a full house.

Stephe and Jack had the nauseating task of emptying out their parents' office on the second floor so it could be converted into a bedroom for the Guttierezes. They spent days boxing up files and their parents' personal effects. Stephe lost it when he found a file of all his old schoolwork, neatly arranged in a folder in Diane's desk drawer. Awards, trophies, nicknacks and bits of their parent's lives were placed in boxes and stacked in the garage.

Inez wound up being a fantastic cook and quickly put the kitchen into order for herself. Fantastic El Salvadorean food was served up every night. Instead of a bowl of cereal in front of the TV, dinner became a feast for seven people in the dining room. It was heavenly, in its own way. It helped make the loneliness more bearable.

Frank and Bob Enwright took Stephen and Diane's bedroom at the top of the house, which, at first, hurt Stephe's feelings. But they had to sleep somewhere; everyone had to help out.

All four guests were retired, so the house was always full of people. Stephe couldn't imagine facing the summer alone, and fortunately he didn't have to. Margery was still working nights and sleeping during the day so everyone had to be quiet; the only one to not get the memo was Coal, who barked incessantly.

Frank and Bob: were fascinating to Stephe. The Enwrights had been married until the Trump Administration and Supreme Court overturned gay marriage in 2020.

Stephe knew he was gay by the time he was five years old but had never told a soul; he wondered if he'd ever tell anyone. He nearly plotzed when Bob and Frank came to live with them at 472 Liberty Street. They were not the least bit alluring to him, in their late-60s, but he quivered at night knowing two gay married men shared a bed upstairs and clearly loved each other. Bob and Frank Enwright had had a Victorian house on Oak Street—lost in the fire, along with priceless furnishings, antiques—everything.

Stephe hung around Bob and Frank a lot, asking questions about their relationship, forming in his mind, at last, the picture that he could be gay and still turn out okay.

Stephe came out to Bob and Frank one day in August. Scared to death, he decided to tell them he was gay. They chuckled. They already knew. They assured him his secret would be safe with them. He was able to ask questions. How did they meet? What was it like? How did it work now that gay marriage was outlawed again?

They were around in the 1970s, in the heyday of the Castro when it was gay men everywhere and sex at the drop of a hat.

"You could pick someone up in line at the grocery store," Frank winked. "It was a free-for-all. But then came AIDS. And then in the '90s all these straight people began moving into the neighborhood. No offense to your family."

Bob and Frank were a class act. They'd say just enough to tease and titillate Stephe, but never crossed the line into gross or inappropriate.

By September it was time to go back to school. Jack got accepted into Stanford, and thus began his commute every day to Palo Alto. Caltrain still wasn't back in service yet, but fleets of buses took up the slack. It was over an hour each way, but Jack said he didn't mind. He could study on the bus.

Mission High School opened its battered doors on September 5th. Portable trailers were set up in the play field behind the school, used in conjunction with the parts of the high school that were undamaged. It was crowded and awkward. But Stephe was glad to go back; to begin his sophomore year.

Dolores Park, across the street, had been turned into a tent city, housing two thousand homeless refugees.

Stephe didn't see much of his friend Ben anymore. They just didn't see eye to eye; Ben was turning into quite the homophobe. He was way into sports and girls and Stephe just didn't see any future in it. So he was painfully shy of friends. He just kept his head down and did his schoolwork and stayed out of trouble.

Frank and Bob were his closest friends that year.

Chapter 3

Large swaths of the city had to be rebuilt: South of Market, the Mission, Haight Ashbury. Gone were the wooden Victorians, to be replaced with mid-rise skyscrapers, mixed use buildings. They built upwards. San Francisco quickly started to look like Vancouver's West End, with block after block of terraced apartment buildings.

San Francisco had long been starved for housing, with the highest rents in the country—worse, even, than New York. It is a city only seven miles wide and seven miles long, with mostly single-family houses. Since the mid-1990s, the housing crunch began to change San Francisco. What had been the country's most diverse and off-beat city became increasingly sterile as working people were forced out of their rent-controlled apartments and houses. By the 2000s only the very rich could afford the city. By 2020 the chief complaint was that the city had lost its character to tech sector trust-fund kids. Venerable restaurants and charming institutions were being priced out at an alarming rate.

The post-quake rebuilding fixed the city's greatest problem—housing—and then some. Commercial space was more profitable, but by building up, and by quintupling the housing supply with mid-rise condos and apartments, suddenly rents came down. Many people chose to move away, anxious to fight their mourning and to start new lives elsewhere. But new people flooded into the city. By 2024, San Francisco became a boom town once more.

By age fifteen, Stephe was a junior in high school.

Pedro and Inez moved into new housing in November of 2023, Frank and Bob in December. The house was empty again—just in time for Christmas.

Jack got a job waiting tables at night after school.

Being gay in high school in San Francisco in the year 2023 was no big deal, but Stephe didn't feel any compulsion to be loudly out of the closet. He still hadn't told anyone beside Frank and Bob, nor did he feel any real connection to the LGBT students at school. For one thing, he liked men in their twenties and thirties with beards and hairy bodies. So his fellow high schoolers were of only slight interest to him, as were the generally elderly gay and tattooed residents of the Castro District.

Gay life in the rest of America was not going well, following the repeal of gay marriage by the U.S. Supreme Court. Gay bashings were up. Religious groups were politically stronger and had won the right to discriminate openly against gays and lesbians in most states.

But Stephe was fairly insulated against this in San Francisco, and further so being in the Castro, the gayest neighborhood in the country since the 1970s. Its status as thus had diminished during the housing crunch. More and more straight families— including Stephe's own—moved into the almost exclusively gay neighborhood starting in the 1990s. It was still a haven for gay tourists. The notorious Beck's Lodge on Market Street was demolished in 2020 and became a Whole Foods, but plenty of tourists came to vacation there and older gay men remained.

There was the old joke about what do you call two men holding hands in the Castro? Tourists.

Stephe found a new best friend named Henry Donecki. He was straight, but somehow they got along well. Sandy-haired and stocky, Henry already shaved once a week. They'd hang out after school, and had several classes together. Stephe was kind of in love with Henry, but of course couldn't say so to him. It would be friendship suicide! Henry clearly liked girls—a lot.

One fall day, when he was fifteen, after the Guttierezes had moved out, Stephe and Henry were in Stephe's room late on a Wednesday night. Sitting on Stephe's bed, they'd played on their phones until they were sick of it and the room was dark.

"We could play Truth or Dare," Henry suggested.

"Truth," Stephe said quickly.

"Who do you have a crush on?" Henry asked.

Stephe lied, "Kaylee Aguilar."

"Aguilar!" Henry exclaimed. "Hah! She's a skank!"

"She is not!" Stephe rebutted. "Your turn. Who do *you* have a crush on?"

"Definitely . . . Mrs. Chong," Henry replied, waiting for Stephe to laugh. Mrs. Chong, their math teacher, was in her sixties and, frankly, pretty gross. She was not well-liked at Mission High.

"Gimme a break. Who do you really like?"

"Melanie Groubert." She was a cheerleader and stacked to the gills. "She's got really nice tits."

"Have you ever talked to her?" Stephe asked.

"Fuck, no! Jesus, she wouldn't even know who I am! Truth or dare?" Henry continued.

"Dare."

"I dare you to . . . take off your pants!"

Stephe's heart fluttered in his chest. "C'mon," he whined. It was so cheesy. But as horrified as he was, he was also intrigued.

"No, you have to do it!"

Stephe stood up, undid his trousers and stepped out of them, leaving them on the floor of his room. He felt flushed and foolish. He sat back down on the bed next to Henry in his purple underwear and white socks.

"Truth or dare," he declared.

"Dare."

"Off!" Stephe said, beckoning at Henry's jeans. Stephe had gotten plenty of glimpses of Henry in the showers in P.E. at school. He knew Henry's body, his stout frame and small wrinkled penis in a sea of blonde hair. Henry stepped out of his jeans defiantly and sat back down on the bed in white Fruit of the Loom underwear.

"Truth or dare," Henry asked.

"Truth!" Stephe responded quickly.

"Have you ever made out with a girl? Kissed? Touched a tit?" Henry challenged.

"No," Stephe answered. "Truth or Dare?"

"Truth," Henry replied.

"Same question."

Henry sighed. "Yes. Natalie Gardner. Last year. We French-kissed at Melody Randwick's party. Once."

"What was it like?" Stephe asked, intrigued.

"Soft, mostly," Henry replied. "It was real quick."

"Have you ever gotten a hard-on in school?" Stephe asked, not even bothering to ask if it was Truth or Dare, or even if it was his turn.

"Shit, yeah!" Henry replied. "Last week in science class I

had a solid boner for twenty minutes, I swear! I had to leave my jacket in my lap!"

"Me, too," Stephe admitted, enthralled at the thought. "It's embarrassing. I pictured someone touching it with their fingers, and I got so excited, it was rock hard and wouldn't go down."

"Have you ejaculated?" Henry asked. "I have. Every day, now that I've found out how."

"Me, too," Stephe answered softly. "First time was a hell of a surprise, but I figured out what it was and immediately did it again."

Henry laughed. "Yeah. It's a wonder I ever leave the house!"

Stephe was horrified and thrilled and grateful, all at once. He'd never had a conversation like this with anyone— not even Jack.

"Truth or Dare?" Henry suddenly asked.

"Dare," Stephe slowly replied.

Henry paused before simply saying "Underwear," and tilting his head in the direction of Stephe's midsection in the darkened room.

Stephe's heart started thumping wildly in his chest. Was this really happening?

He did as he was told. He stood and slithered out of his underwear and quickly sat back down on the bed, feeling the cool bedspread on his bare butt and under his balls. *Please, God, don't let me get a boner!* he thought. His throat and mouth were suddenly dry.

"T or D?" he asked Henry.

"D."

Stephe pointed to Henry's tighty-whities with a thrill.

Without saying a word Henry jumped up, shed his Fruit of the Looms and sat back down on the bed next to Stephe, still wearing his socks but naked from the waist down.

It was murky in the room. Stephe, heart pounding madly, wished he'd turned on a light. But he couldn't now. He glanced at Henry's cock and balls and blonde hair just a foot away from him: They looked bigger than in the gym here in the gloom. His own dick gave a little jump and started filling with blood. He covered his midsection with his hands.

"No fair," Henry said, and reached over and brushed Stephe's hands away from hiding his own crotch, and, in doing so, brushed Stephe's dick with his fingers. That was all it took. Stephe's penis jumped to full attention at the accidental touch—was it an accident? He sat there with his shoulders lowered, looking down at the rug, cock at full height.

He heard Henry breathe next to him and longed to touch his friend, longed to do many things he'd thought of for so long.

Finally he dared to glance to his right and what he saw thrilled him to the core of his being. Henry had an erection, too.

They sat there for a minute in identical condition; arms down, shoulder's hunched, heads down. Henry's thigh was just a few inches to the right of Stephe; he could feel the heat of his friend's leg. He didn't dare move, yet he knew he had to do something. He took a dry swallow; his parched throat made a loud clicking sound in the room. He moved his right leg over until it came in contact with Henry's bare left leg and at the touch an electricity jolted through him.

Henry pressed his leg too. Just a bit.

Stephe couldn't breathe.

Henry slowly, tentatively, brought his left hand up and began to caress Stephe's erection with the tips of his cool fingers and Stephe thought he would explode. He did breathe then; ragged and deep, as Henry, overcoming his shyness, traced his fingers up and down Stephe's cock. When he ran his fingers over Stephe's scrotum the feeling was nearly unbearable—a sweet, ticklish charge of sensations that drove Stephe mad with pleasure.

Stephe's shoulders were up; his hands pressing down onto the edge of the bed, arms locked, hips thrust up as Henry became bolder. His breathing was ragged as he grabbed Stephe's cock harder and began to become confident in his touch.

Even though the sensations were overpowering, Stephe turned his attention to Henry, and with his right hand, gently reached over and touched another man's penis for the first time in his life. The sensation was startling: Dry, soft and pliant, but Henry's erection pounded to full force and Stephe felt an incredible thrill. He traced his fingers around a startlingly large head, up and down the shaft and cupped Henry's balls. Henry gasped.

The two fifteen-year-olds, not looking each other in the eye, continued to pleasure each other until finally Henry could hold off no more; Stephe, who by now was well-versed in bringing himself to climax, turned his efforts to Henry and, within seconds, Henry began shuddering and let go of a long stream of sperm.

"Oh, God," Henry said, and he ripped his hand away from Stephe's midsection.

Henry sat up straight and, shaking his head as though with a tic, grabbed his underwear from the floor and stood, wiping himself.

Stephe began stroking himself hoping to follow suit but Henry hurriedly pulled his now-sticky underwear on and released the waistband into place with a loud snap. He grabbed his pants, pulled them on and then snatched up his Nike's. He needed to sit back down to put them on which he did at the far edge of the bed and, without saying a word, fled the darkened room.

In shock, his own erection forgotten, Stephe felt sick in the pit of his stomach as he heard Henry's footfalls down the old staircase and the slam of the front door.

The next day at school was dark and heavy for Stephe. He and Henry typically sat next to each other in second period Algebra class and would usually take turns texting nasty comments about Mrs. Chong and her tits. On this day, with a resolute and pale look on his face, Henry charged past his usual desk, stomped to the rear of the room, and sat down alone. Stephe was horrified.

After Henry had left the night before, Stephe had gone to bed early in a confusion of excitement and despair. Oh, the things he had wanted to do with Henry! The things that he *had done* with Henry—wonderful things! He brought himself off twice under the covers, reliving every touch, every caress—replaying it step by step in his mind so he'd never forget. But Henry's reaction left him feeling sick and ugly.

What had he done wrong?

Today, he recounted everything that had happened and he was three-quarters through his day by the time he had it fixed clearly in his mind: Henry had initiated the whole encounter. That assurance just left him more confused and alone than ever.

Henry didn't even show up to gym class that day. On subsequent days he completely ignored Stephe and struck up loud and obnoxious friendships with Chuck Meeker and Ross Phelan—two jocks they used to make fun of together.

Henry never acknowledged Stephe again.

After his experience with Henry, Stephe was cloven in two. He had sexual desires. He not only just *had* them; they were attenuated to a fever pitch. A fifteen-year-old boy doesn't think of much besides sex. Stephe was no exception, but he had no outlet for it. He was hurt by Henry and afraid of being hurt again. There was no one he could talk to about these issues; no way to get his needs met. So he stayed isolated.

What he really wanted was a man to love and be loved by—the relationship Bob and Frank had. He'd dream Cinderella dreams of his future happiness with a man. The loss of his parents just made it worse. He felt empty inside. Bereft.

He was doing well enough in school; his grades were good, but the subjects were not very interesting to him.

In 2023 he became best friends with a girl named Nona Ruiz. She had lost her mother in the earthquake and lived with a very strict father, Francisco. She was second generation Guatemalan on her father's side. Nona had black hair and blue eyes, hair she kept in a short bob with bangs. She was in Stephe's English class, but they'd never spoken. They formally met one day on the 33 Stanyan bus; Stephe was on his way back from Mission Animal Hospital to pick up some Clavamox for Lilo the cat, and he recognized Nona from class. Nona invited him to sit with her.

There were some loud kids in the back of the bus playing music and being obnoxious.

"Do you not despair for the future?" Nona queried.

"I weep," Stephe answered.

"How are you getting along in English?"

"Super boring. English is my best subject, but I don't find it particularly challenging."

"Me either," Nona responded.

"I like it best when we have writing assignments. Just sitting around reading books gets a little dry."

"Are you going to go to college?" Nona asked. "I'm hoping for Berkeley, if I can swing it."

"That's where I want to go, too," Stephe replied. "I suppose I'd major in English, but what would that do for getting a well-paid job? I'm also kind of interested in Political Science."

"Poli Sci would get me down. Politics in this place has gone haywire. I mean, after seven years of dumpster fire that is the Trump administration, there's not much left to learn about."

"That's true. I'm definitely not a fan."

"This became a shithole country years ago," Nona continued. "They even tried to come after my father's citizenship. He was born here, for Christ's sake. He doesn't even speak Spanish."

They were coming up on Castro Street.

"You wanna go get coffee?" she asked.

"Sure!" Stephe replied.

They got off at Walgreen's and walked back to the Starbucks which had taken over the entire corner of the building at 18th Street. They went in and ordered, and then sat and talked. Politics and English. Nona was unbelievably cool. She seemed to know something about everything, but she wasn't uppity about it. Stephe could tell that, like himself, she had a brain that worked into overtime. She seemed much older than fifteen years of age.

They began hanging out after that, but they had a

problem. She seemed interested in Stephe—romantically so. Stephe avoided thinking about it, but he couldn't sidestep the issue forever. It was getting in the way of their friendship, which, he hoped, wouldn't end.

He needed to tell her he was gay.

He'd dropped a few hints, but they sounded lame to him even as he said them. It wasn't going to work that way.

Stephe had never told anyone he was gay, except Bob and Frank, and that had been easy. Nona was cool; he knew that. He'd engineered conversations on the topic and sussed her out. She was good. But he had to tell her.

Finally one day in the cafeteria at Mission High, with beating heart and fear in his belly, quietly so as not to be overheard, he revealed that he was gay.

"No shit?" she said, leaning back. "Wow. Okay." And that was the end of that. They remained friends, hanging out after school, eating dinner in the Castro when they could afford it. Nona was the funniest person Stephe knew—and smart! Not many people could outthink Stephe, but Nona ran circles around him.

They'd talk for hours about men and boys, once Stephe came out to her. Nona never seemed to have crushes on high school boys; like Stephe, she was interested in older men.

One day he told her about Henry. He wasn't going to say who, but she wormed it out of him.

"And he initiated it?" she asked.

"Well, pretty much. He told me to take off my pants; he grabbed my dick first."

"He's either a closet case," she said, "or maybe he's totally straight and just needed to get his rocks off."

"Either way, it kinda messed me up," Stephe complained. "It left a bad taste in my mouth."

Nona snickered. Stephe gave her a playful shove.

"You know what I mean." Stephe continued, "I think about sex all the time, but I don't want to get brushed off like that again. I couldn't handle it. We were good friends, and then he went and completely cut me out."

"You just need to have sex. Without expectation, without someone who's a closet case."

"There's just no guys here at school who are both gay and the least bit interesting to me."

"What about Tim LaGrande?" Nona asked and then giggled.

Tim was the school's most flaming gay guy, effeminate to the point of being awkward. As he was unlocking his bike the other day, Stephe and Nona had observed some girls snickering at Tim and he responded "SSsssssuck my dyick." They had both burst out laughing.

"I keep hoping for Dean Barker," Stephe mused. Nona just sighed and shook her head.

Dean Barker was nineteen and bearded; he'd been held back a year. Total bear jock, drove a Ford pick-up and was God to Stephe. But hopelessly straight. Massive frame, six foot two, played football and baseball. Stephe had him in gym class and once, just once, showered next to him and checked out his hairy butt and cock. Dean kind of started to notice, so Stephe pretended to get soap in his eye.

"If only there was a way to get him drunk," Nona mused. "You might have a shot then."

Stephe had never spoken to Dean—never had the courage.

"You finally going to go to the LGBT ice cream social on Thursday? I keep telling you you need to go." It had been Nona's idea for months that Stephe establish some good gay contacts, and to be more "out" at school.

"Yeah. I think I'm going to give it a try."

"Good boy," she said, patting his knee.

The next Thursday he decided to attend. It was a big, big step for him, and he was nervous. But he went. They met after school at the newly opened Ben & Jerry's on Castro. Seven or eight gay students would push the tables together and enjoy their ice cream. He was surprised and a little disappointed that he already knew everyone there to one degree or other. There were a few people he liked, a few angry lesbians he didn't, and being seen out in the LGBT group meant he was officially out at school. No big deal; a few guys stopped talking to him and a few girls started. By this time, Ben had stopped talking to him completely.

Stephe realized he should come out to Jack and Margery. Jack had always been pretty cool—Stephe knew he had gay friends—but Margery was a mystery. She was a closet case as far as anyone could tell; he and Jack would talk about the likelihood that Margery was a lesbian but too fearful to acknowledge it, even to herself.

With Mom and Dad gone, there was just too much aloneness; he couldn't bear the thought of losing Jack by being gay. His rational mind told him it would be fine. But his irrational mind screamed for attention. He was already an orphan— would he lose his only brother, too?

He'd already come out at school. And while Jack wasn't in the habit of hanging around with high schoolers, what if he had already heard from someone else? Stephe didn't want it to go down that way.

He stewed over it for several days, barely able to eat. He was nervous every time he saw Jack around the house when Jack wasn't commuting back and forth to Stanford or working.

Finally, it was a Saturday night. Margery was at work at the hospital; Jack was in his room, studying.

Stephe decided it was now or never.

He went into Jack's bedroom right across the hall from his own, while Jack was writing on his laptop at the desk, in a pool of light from a single lamp and the light of the screen; several heavy textbooks lay open on his desk and one on his lap.

"How's it going?" Stephe asked, standing awkwardly next to him.

"Boring as fuck," Jack said, closing and tossing a book back onto the stack. "How you doing?"

"I'm okay," he replied hesitantly.

"What's it like at school? I walked around the other day. The place is unrecognizable with all the construction."

"It's good," Stephe replied. "I don't really hang with anybody except Nona."

"What happened to that creep, Henry?" Jack asked. "I don't see him anymore."

"He just sort of," Stephe fumbled for words, "moved on, I guess."

"I always thought he looked kinda like a sawed-off loser," Jack shot back.

With a beautiful big-headed dick, thought Stephe.

"Jack, there's something I need to tell you," Stephe began. "I have to tell you. But I'm worried how you're going to take it."

"What?" Jack sat up, looking concerned.

"Well . . . I'm gay," Stephe said, looking down at the rug, feeling woozy as he stood.

"I know that, stupid!" Jack said with a gentle sigh.

Stephe was shocked and quickly looked up to Jack's blue

eyes. "You do?"

"Sure. I've always known."

"Really?" Stephe asked again.

"Well, let me think. Who had a Princess Leia doll until he was eight years old?" Jack asked lightly.

Stephe was stunned. "Are you cool with it?" Stephe blurted out. "I guess I really need you to be cool with it; after losing Mom and Dad, you're all I have left, and I've come out at school—everybody knows—and I didn't want you to hear about it from someone else."

"Yeah, I'm cool with it," Jack responded. "You know I'm friends with lots of gay guys. Were you actually worried about me?

"Well, a little. Like I said, you're all I have left."

"I'm sorry you had to sweat it, little brother. Naw, we're good. Should we hug it out?"

Jack stood, and they hugged.

"Thank you," Stephe said, muffled in his brother's shoulder.

"Naw, thank *you*. I'm glad you told me." He thumped Stephe's back and they parted. Jack sat down again. "Question is, does Margery know?"

"Aw, hell no!" answered Stephe. "I don't know if I should tell her. With her, I really wouldn't know what to expect."

"Yeah, you could trigger her," Jack answered with a slight laugh. "The truth is, we don't know about dear Margery. I really think she's a closet case. She's probably very conflicted."

"I know. But I feel like she should be told. Just like with you, I don't want her to hear it from someone else."

"Well, *I'm* not going to tell her," Jack said, quietly but firmly.

"I know. And I should tell her alone," Stephe responded. "I wouldn't want her to feel ganged up on."

"That may be, but if you want me there with you, I'll do it," Jack offered.

"Thanks. I guess I have to decide."

"Well, better make it quick, before you start bringing boyfriends home. Speaking of . . . do you have a boyfriend?" Jack asked.

"No, not by a long shot!"

"Nobody at school strikes your fancy? Hell, we're in the middle of the Castro, you oughta make out like a bandit!" Jack laughed.

"Naw, there's no gay guys at school I'm really into," Stephe admitted. "I could totally go for Dean Barker, but he's as straight as they come."

"Dean! Is he still there?" Jack was stunned. "Jesus, he was in my English class. He can barely read and write. You can do better than that. But he's so dumb, you could probably fool him into a blowjob."

Stephe blushed. He couldn't believe he was discussing Dean Barker in such terms with his own brother. It felt wonderful.

"Could I?" he asked hopefully.

Jack reached out and gave him a backhanded slap to the thigh. "Don't go getting any ideas; it's not nice to tease the straight people. Have you had any. . . experiences? You're a little young, I don't want you to get into trouble."

"I just had touchy-feelies. Once. It ended badly."

"Huh. Well, you're only fifteen. Don't rush into anything. I didn't go there until I was nineteen—damn near killed me! My hormones were off the charts."

"Yeah. I'm there," Stephe admitted. "But I don't know, I'm waiting for something good."

"Do that. People who play around too early are kinda

messed up for life, y'know what I mean? And for God's sake, stay safe!"

"I will. I can't imagine I'll ever get laid." Stephe shook his head and declared, "I'm dyin'."

"Well I'm glad you told me. If you have any questions or need advice—not that I'm so experienced—but you let me know, okay?"

"'Kay. Thanks, Jack. It really helped, having Bob and Frank here. They taught me a lot. I told them awhile back . . . and they already knew. "

"Yeah, I wondered about that. They're really nice guys. We were lucky, having cool people stay with us. I'm glad it worked out." He chucked him on the shoulder. "Now, I gotta study," Jack said. "You be careful out there. And let me know what you decide about Margery."

Stephe went back to his room and laid on the bed, on his back, his hands behind his head. He felt glorious. He basked in his accomplishment for several minutes before texting Nona: "I did it. Jack was so cool!"

"Yay! Congrats! I told you he'd be okay"

"He suggests Dean Barker's so dumb I could fool him into a BJ. Think I could?"

Nona replied, "Grrrrr. Don't go there!"

Stephe texted, "I know. This feels good."

"Total congrats. I'm proud of you!"

"Thanks!" Stephe sent in reply.

Margery Johnson remained a mystery. Despite glee at his success with Jack, Stephe wondered how vital it was to come out to Marge. She wasn't likely to hear high school gossip. Jack was right; it could seriously trigger her. People who were confused about their own sexuality were usually the ones with the most extreme reactions.

He just kept it to himself for a few weeks.

One Monday late evening, around 7:30, walking back from Nona's at 16th and Dolores Streets, he got his first cutting reminder of the realities of this world. Making his way through Dolores Park at dusk—the tent city had finally been cleared and it was a park again—as he'd done so many times before, he was quickly surrounded by three guys.

"Hey faggot," one of them said, and all three moved to converge on him. Stephe had been so lost in thought he didn't notice it was happening until he heard the word "faggot." He looked up startled; it was too dark to get a good look at the guys, but two of them were sizeably bigger than he and the smallest—apparently the leader—grabbed Stephe by the front of his shirt and jerked him forward, almost pulling him off his feet.

"Are you a faggot?" he hissed, and Stephe could smell beer on his breath. They seemed somewhat older than him... college age, maybe.

"N-n-n-no," he stammered weakly, his heart hammering in his chest. Even his word "no" sounded gay to him, and through his fear he also felt shame at his weak lie.

The leader kicked at Stephe's left leg and pulled him to the ground by his shirt.

All three guys pounced.

The attack was an eternity of pain and fear. Each punch to the head was an explosion of light and pain. Stephe had never felt so helpless in his life.

Two of the men were beating his face and ears, while the third kicked methodically, first in Stephe's backside and kidneys, then he came around and tried to land several to Stephe's stomach. As Stephe curled into the fetal position, the attacker couldn't land but one or two kicks to his actual belly; those that did knocked the wind out of him and made him retch. But he finally got his knees up so the kicks just landed on his shins and the guy, frustrated, started stomping on Stephe's thighs with his boots.

The beatings to his face and head were like claps of thunder, each individual blow hurting less and less as the pain became general, systemic. Overpowering.

After less than a minute the attack was done, and they ran off, laughing and high-fiving each other, leaving Stephe curled on the ground in agony. He vomited heavily on the grass.

When he could finally move, he painfully crouched on all fours, looking wildly around to make sure they were gone. Through tears—or was it blood?—he could make out other people in the park, under the streetlights, walking along as if nothing was wrong; while he waited for more blows to come. But his attackers were gone.

Carefully he got to his feet. The pain was excruciating. He was able to stand, dizzy and swaying and tasting blood in his mouth. Every part of his head hurt. He put his hand to his forehead and felt blood. His wallet and phone were still in his pockets. It hadn't even been a mugging.

He'd just been queer bashed.

He didn't know what to do. Should he call the police? Walk to Nona's? Or walk home? He was equidistant between Nona's and 472 Liberty Street, and he wanted to quickly get out of the park. He staggered toward the closest light standard and into the pool of light. Several homeless people were strewn about, but none paid him any attention.

He realized dully that he was headed for home so that was the direction he maintained. He turned to the right and headed back to 18th Street. More people there; he'd feel safer. Walking slowly, back into darkness, he finally reached the sidewalk at 18th and Church Street and the Muni streetcar tracks. He was directly in front of his high school, all lit up and looking like a normal construction site.

Blood was coming out of his head. His nose, most likely. Despite the cool fog he took off his overshirt and blotted his face, his head still pounding and a ringing in his ears. The shirt came away covered in blood.

As he made his way up 18th Street he began to encounter people and restaurants and lights and sounds. People stared at him in a ghastly way, but he kept his eyes down and stomped up the hill to his house.

He kept thinking he was being followed, kept thinking they'd come back to finish the job, and everything felt haunted to him. He was crying by the time he opened the door to 472 Liberty.

Margery was in the kitchen with a cup of camomile tea and her iPad when he staggered into the bright light of the room.

"Oh my God!" she cried and leapt to her feet. "What in the *world*? Are you all right? What *happened?*"

"I . . . I just got queer bashed," Stephe cried. In his pain and shock he realized he'd just outed himself to Margery. But if she picked up on it, she didn't let on. She held him by his arms at arm's length for the briefest of moments—rare warmth for her—and immediately sprang to the sink and began running the hot water. "Come over here so I can get a good look at you," she said. Stephe, suddenly tired, just plunked himself down at the kitchen table and put what remained of his head into his hands and sobbed.

Margery got a white dishtowel soaking with hot water and sat down next to him.

"Let me see."

She began blotting under his nose and around his eyes, the towel coming back so alarmingly red, Stephe felt as though he might faint. She cleaned up his face and tutted and murmured, "I'm so sorry, Stephe. I'm so sorry. Awww. Tsk."

Finally, businesslike, she asked, "Tell me where you're hurt; tell me where they hit you."

"My head!" Stephe responded angrily. "And my chest, and they kicked my legs and stomach. I threw up."

"Did you call the police?"

"No. I was in the park, it was dark. I couldn't see who it was."

"You *have* to call the police!"

"Okay, I will, I just wanted to get home first," he protested.

"I think your nose is broken and you're going to need stitches."

"Which do I do first?" Stephe asked impatiently.

"Let's get you to Davies and make sure you're all right. We can call 9-1-1 while we're waiting."

With no hesitation Margery packed up her iPad, grabbed her coat and called an Uber. They went to Davies Hospital just up the road. She checked Stephe in to Emergency. Davies was a small hospital but the closest one. Besides, Margery worked there so she knew Palacio who was manning the admittance desk in the ER.

"Awww, honey," said Palacio as she took his insurance card.

Stephe finally called 9-1-1 while they were waiting.

"9-1-1. Your emergency please?" said the voice at the other end of the line.

"My name is Stephen Stafford and I've just been assaulted and beaten up."

"Where are you located?" the voice asked.

"I'm at Davies ER; the attack happened in Dolores Park about twenty minutes ago."

"Are you in physical danger right now?"

"No, I'm safe, at the hospital. I guess I need stitches."

"We'll send someone to take a statement."

"Thank you," Stephe replied.

The ER was busy that night. An extremely drunk man named Delmer was giving them hell and he stank; his colostomy bag had come undone and he was fighting off the nurses.

Two SFPD officers, a man and a woman, showed up in about thirty minutes to take Stephe's statement. At pain to recount his experience, he did what he could. In no way could he describe his assailants; it was too dark and they wore hoodies. Finally the police gave him a case number and encouraged him to register his assault with CUAV—Community United Against Violence—an LGBT watchdog group that kept track of such attacks.

The police left, wished him well, and that was that. They were friendly and concerned, but formal and businesslike.

Stephe waited about an hour with Margery, the two not saying much to each other, but her muttering "I'm so sorry" a few times, looking up from her iPad. Pent up adrenaline pushed him into an odd euphoric state for a few moments; he'd been through something awful but he survived! He called Nona.

"I just got queer bashed in Dolores Park."

"Oh my God, are you all right? Where are you?"

"I'm waiting in the ER at Davies. Margery is with me. The police just left."

"*Jesus!* What did they do to you? What happened? Are you okay?"

Stephe recounted the tale again; it was all becoming a blur.

"So I'm bruised all over and have a bloody nose and a gash on my forehead. Margery says I'm going to have two black eyes."

"Jesus," Nona said again. "Do you want me to come be there with you?"

Stephe did. But he didn't want to be a pain. It was close to 9:45 p.m. on a Monday night. "Naw, I'm okay. It's a school night and I don't know how long this'll take."

"Well, I'm so sorry! You gotta write it up to CUAV; promise me you'll do that."

"That's what the police said, too, so I will do it tomorrow," Stephe promised.

"Send me a picture. I want to see what the bastards did to you!"

Stephe hadn't thought to look at himself in a mirror. He was worried at what he might find, but he said, "Just a sec," and took a selfie. He texted it to Nona and tried not looking at it—except he caught a slight glance and it was bad.

"Mother fuck!" Nona exclaimed.

"I haven't looked. I don't want to know."

"Oh, you're as handsome as ever," Nona said reassuringly. "Only you look like you've just had work done. You should put it on Facebook. Call me when they release you, okay? I'll be up."

"'Kay. I will."

"I love you."

"I love you too. I'll call you when I get back home. I think I don't want to go to school tomorrow," Stephe said.

"Call me. Good luck. And Stephe; I'm so sorry!"

It was about 10:05 once Stephe was admitted into the exam room; they asked him questions, first having him get out of his clothes and into a hospital gown so they could examine the rapidly forming bruises on his legs, buttocks and torso. He had a broken nose, two black eyes, and a gash over his left eye requiring thirteen stitches. They numbed the site and stitched him up. The process took about a quarter of an hour and he was released with some Vicodin and instructions on how to check for signs of concussion. Margery assured them she was on it. They all knew Marge, so Stephe felt like a VIP.

The took an Uber back to Liberty Street and Stephe headed for bed, the Vicodin making him feel warm all over.

He took another selfie, with his stitches covered in a bandage and his eyes getting darker by the minute. He posted it on Facebook and Instagram, immediately getting "likes" and messages of sympathy and anger. Jack Messengered him from work, asking if he was okay.

Once again in bed, the Vicodin calm competed with the horrible feelings in his stomach. He felt so vulnerable. He'd been sorely mistreated and hadn't even seen it coming. He finally fell asleep and had horrible dreams of falling. Repeatedly.

True to his word, he stayed home from Mission High the next day, fielding numerous texts from people at school asking if he was all right, asking what happened. So many that he resorted to just cutting and pasting the text. He filed his case with CUAV online.

The next day, Wednesday, he was a minor celebrity at

school. His eyes had blackened to the point that he looked like a raccoon. He even caught Henry noticing him, although he said nothing. The bruises continued to hurt, but there was no permanent damage, just aches and pains. He felt like an old man at fifteen years of age.

It took a toll on his confidence though. Walking at night forever bothered him. He steered clear of Dolores Park for a long time after that evening, wondering how he could so casually have ignored the dangers for so long.

Word filtered through of other gay bashings around the neighborhood, roughly matching the descriptions of his assailants. People began carrying police whistles again, as they did when bashings were up.

School continued apace after the excitement was over. Stephe continued to get good grades in everything except math. He and Nona would study together most days at his place or hers, or at Harvey Milk Library on 15th. They had mostly the same classes and would race to see who could get their homework done first. Nona usually won; Stephe started calling her Hermione Granger, which she said she hated but Stephe figured she actually loved. She was able to help him with his math somewhat, enough to keep his grades from tanking.

By February, 2024, his birthday month, he was sixteen and starting to grow facial hair. Not much; Margery was forever after him to start shaving but he liked the look and refused. It was coming in reddish-blond and Stephe was fiercely proud of it.

The highlight of his sixteenth year was learning how to drive. They had an old plug-in Prius in the tiny garage and Stephe delighted in driving. There was not much use for a car in San Francisco; in fact, cars were more of a liability with some of the worst parking in the country. But he'd drive when he could, and he loved it. He was saddened that autonomous cars were becoming the norm; it just wasn't fun anymore.

Nona was determined not to be outdone, so she took a driving course, too, even though she didn't have a car. She used the Prius with Margery's reluctant approval, and passed with flying colors.

They'd drive around a lot. Trips to Costco, Half Moon Bay, Marin Headlands, Berkeley Hills.

Stephe and Nona went to an anime convention in San Jose, mostly to harsh on the other geeks, but they got their pictures taken with the hordes in their cosplay get-ups. Ultimately, though, they got into it. Nona was dressed as a faery queen and Stephe as a Pikachu. It was fun after all; it wound up being worth their time.

They'd often drive out to Lafayette and walk around the reservoir talking about school or boys. Nona claimed to have finally lost her virginity to a guy named Curtis. They'd gone out a few times—Stephe met him and found him distant and possibly gay—and she described the night in detail to Stephe. It hurt, she said, and didn't last very long. Nona wanted to be in love with Curtis, but he quickly became distant and pushed her away. Nona was devastated.

Chapter 4

When he was seventeen, in 2025, Stephe got a job at Cliff's Variety & Hardware Store on Castro Street. Cliff's was an institution in the neighborhood. Previously an old music box theatre, the hardware store had been a fixture since 1936. He was hired as a stock boy and floor runner. It wasn't exciting to him, but he enjoyed working with people.

The store was divided into two sections: hardware and fabric. The fabric section next door was presided over by a man in a kilt named Paul, and it sold cutesie cushions, knick-knacks and soaps, tassels and feather boas—it was where drag queens went to get their kit on.

The main hardware section had everything from paint to lumber, kitchen supplies to children's games.

Stephe worked most afternoons after school and on Saturdays, heavily eating into his homework time and Nona time; Nona got a job as an office assistant at a title company and they hardly got a chance to see each other. Still, he managed to keep up with his grades and now had spending money to boot.

Customers at Cliff's could be a real challenge or the greatest fun. Lots of elderly gay men did serious shopping in there, and he got to know many by name. All the older gay men had tattoos and piercings—it was funny; just how their generation was, Stephe guessed. A guy named Al was completely rebuilding his house up at 18th and Douglass Streets and would be in three times a day getting washers, screws, dowels, and buckets of drywall compound. Al would flirt endlessly with Stephe and one day, while Stephe was mixing him some paint Al point blank asked him out for coffee at Starbucks.

Al was in his fifties; shaved head, large plug holes in each ear, tattoos on his arms and knuckles and not that bad to look at. On a lark, Stephe said yes, he'd meet him for coffee. He didn't know why he said yes. He liked Al but wasn't sure he was drawn to him, other than that he was a nice guy.

Stephe had still never had sex. He wanted it badly. Would Al be the one?

He took a lot of his frustrations out online. Most people wouldn't give him the time of day—too young. But he found a few possibilities. All far away, of course. He spent most of his time talking to a twenty-year-old guy named Paul in Portland; they sexted each other like mad, would Skype when Stephe had the house to himself, which was quite often those days. It was the closest thing to sex, and it would have to do. But it was nothing like the reality of warm human touch.

He would also talk to a guy named Drew from school; Drew was out and gay. He was there at the ice cream social Stephe went to that one time. They started talking one day at lunch, and Drew asked Stephe if he was seeing anybody. The answer was obviously no. Drew claimed to have a college-age boyfriend in the East Bay and they hooked up a lot. Stephe didn't believe him, but Drew had pictures. Lots of pictures. In his phone. Carefully, so as to not get caught, he slithered around to Stephe on the bench and showed him.

Well, the pictures didn't lie. Drew was definitely hooking up. They were pretty shocking and Stephe was both fascinated and repulsed.

"I'll text some to you, if you want," Drew offered.

"Sure," Stephe said; why the hell not? He gave Drew his number. Some of the pictures were hot, even though Drew wasn't his type. After that they'd text fairly often, talking about sex. Drew wanted Stephe. But Stephe just wasn't interested in him that way.

Every time Drew hooked up he'd tell Stephe all about it in graphic detail and Stephe ate it all up.

On February 15, 2026, Stephe turned eighteen. He was at that awkward age where his hormones were off the charts. He was looking for love, the Real Deal. It wasn't so much that he was "saving himself for marriage," he just wanted to feel the utz for someone.

He didn't feel the utz for Al. But he was nevertheless finding himself intrigued.

So he met Al at seven o'clock on a Thursday night, chilly, foggy, like nearly every night in San Francisco.

Al was wearing a black jacket and so was Stephe. Al had on a knit cap; Stephe braved the June air with no hat. Stephe ordered his usual double macchiato; Al got a four-shot latte. They sat and talked. Al was out on disability with a bad back; Stephe wondered how that worked, since he was obviously rebuilding a house, but didn't pursue the point, and Al asked after Stephe's schooling. Stephe told him that he was bored with school; he didn't find any gay guys appealing to him.

"You should go to the gay group discussions in Berkeley," Al suggested. "They meet once a week, sort of an encounter group; people of all ages. You'd do well there, I think." It was a splendid idea. Stephe had heard of it, but he hadn't put two and two together to think that he might actually go.

"My lover used to go for ages; it was really good for him."

Lover? It never occurred to Stephe that Al wasn't single. But . . . live and let live.

They had a pretty good conversation, the kind where time slips by quickly. But by eight o'clock it was time for Stephe to get home and do homework; truth be told, he wanted to watch *Dungeons and Dragons* on HBO. It was the season premier at nine. They walked to the curb and without warning Al kissed Stephe on the mouth. Tongue. Pierced. Saliva thicker and cooler than Stephe's own. It shocked him and thrilled him and alarmed him all at once. He felt Al's goatee on his own face and it was woolly and it tickled and it felt really good.

Al grabbed his hand and held it upon the parting of their lips.

"'Bye, kiddo," he said, dropping Stephe's hand, and turning, he quickly left. Stephe stood in amazement watching him walk away in his black jacket and knitted cap, wondering how he felt about what had just happened. It was his first kiss.

He got home and texted Nona.

"Do you want to go there?" she asked.

"I'm really not sure. He suggested I go to the gay rap group at Berkeley. I think I'm gonna."

"Cool! Do it!" she said.

Next he texted Drew and told him about the kiss. Not given to romance, Drew asked if Al sucked his dick.

"Gimme a break! We were just at Starbucks. I'm not sure I want to go there."

"You should go there. Someone needs to break you in before you explode, dude!"

And then he proceeded to regale Stephe with text after text of his latest exploit. Stephe began to wonder if Drew wasn't just taking the piss.

Dungeons and Dragons was as good and epic as it should be; his homework was not.

The following Tuesday, fortunately his night off from Cliff's, Stephe took BART to Berkeley and went to the gay rap group. It was held in a house off campus and he was pretty nervous as he walked through the much warmer air of the East Bay evening. But it felt good and grown-up. He hoped to attend Berkeley in a few months; he was thrilled at the prospect. So it felt good.

Thirteen people were there. Four women and nine men, each ranging from their twenties to thirties, sat in chairs in a circle. Stephe was clearly the youngest in the room, but he was made to feel welcome. They all introduced themselves, and topics of discussion were bandied about: coming out, romance over sluttiness, gay marriage, politics, and grief over loved ones lost in the earthquake.

The group was facilitated by a lesbian named Sandy. She was about twenty-five with blond hair in a cute bob like Nona's; her lover Noelle sat to her left, a heavyset butch woman of about thirty, and the two other women were clean-cut professionals near thirty.

Stephe surveyed the eight other men. One was gorgeous, by the name of Eric; bearded and trim and about twenty-three years old. The others seemed nice and earnest, varying types and ages and handsomeness, but it was to Eric that

Stephe's attention fell. He felt too young to be there but was determined to make a good go of it. They decided on the topics of Coming Out and Politics. Each person told their coming out story. For Stephe, his coming out was to Bob and Frank first, then Jack, and his accidental coming out to his aunt, mentioning that his parents died in the earthquake and he would never know if they knew or not. He said that coming here tonight was just another step in his coming out.

Eric told of his coming out, and Stephe listened intently as he spoke. His father was having a very rough time of it, being a Trump supporter and an anti-gay Republican. That elicited much sympathy from the group.

Once politics came up, the discussion got loud. Everyone was in agreement that the political climate had gotten much worse since the dissolution of gay marriage, and people spoke fervently about the gay persecution in Poland, Hungary, Bulgaria and Austria. They were wondering if it could happen here, too.

"Of course it can happen here!" Sandy boomed. "We've got to be out and proud and stand up."

Stephe told his story of being gay bashed in Dolores Park.

Noelle got it at the BART station in Orinda.

Eric got punched in the stomach leaving a Margaret Cho concert at the Fillmore.

A guy named Steve spoke up and said he'd been bashed, too, in New York.

By a show of hands, six of the thirteen people had experienced violence; nine had been called "faggot" or "dyke" in the last three years.

Stephe caught Eric's eye a time or two, which thrilled him. Eric was his type through and through.

When the meeting ended and people were milling around, Sandy came up and thanked Stephe for coming. "I hope you'll come back, and feel free to bring more people," she said. Stephe was grateful but was also keeping and eye out for Eric, who was hovering over the table with the coffee and donuts.

"Thanks! I will!" Stephe excused himself and headed to the donuts. He wanted to meet Eric; he also wanted the remaining sugar-glazed donut. He wanted both with equal desire.

"How's it going?" he asked Eric, grabbing the last donut.

"Good, thanks," Eric said, filling his cup with coffee from the urn.

"Um . . ." Not sure what to say, Stephe just dove in. "I'm sorry about your dad; that's gotta be tough."

"Yeah. It's not good."

They stood eye to eye. Eric was actually quite a bit taller. Up close he was even more handsome.

"Well," Eric said, "good to meet you. Take care." Swallowing the last of his coffee and tossing the cup, he walked out of the room.

Wednesday, back at Mission High School, was a sad blur. He texted Nona his disappointment on the train home. She was very understanding, but at her pragmatic best: "So, one got away. There's four billion other men in the world."

He still had Al to figure out. The kiss stayed with him. It was his first one. But there was no love; he wasn't sure what to do with it. His hormones were telling him to go for it.

Al asked him at Cliff's that day if he went to Berkeley.

"Yeah," Stephe replied. "It was good. We talked about coming out and about gay bashing."

"All cheerful topics. Did anyone strike your fancy?"

"Oh, yes. This one guy. Wasn't interested, though."

"I find that hard to believe," said Al with a slight wink.

There it was again, Al clearly flirting with him. Stephe looked him over, he in his white t-shirt and Levi's, tattooed arms and fingers. Slightly taller than Stephe with what could only be described as a medium build. When Al walked away, Stephe checked out his butt; looked good.

Stephe manned a cash register and rang up Al's purchases. Al gave him his email address and phone number on a piece of paper.

He was waiting for love and just the right connection, but that was obviously not going to happen. So . . . why not?

He texted Nona. "So there's this guy that comes into Cliff's. I think he wants me to do him. I'm thinking I might."

"Holy shit, for real?" she texted back.

"Yeah. I'm scared."

"Are you sure you want to go through with it? What's his name; what's he like?"

"His name is Al, he's about 55," Stephe texted. "Nice looking. The other night he kissed me with his pierced tongue—my first kiss."

"Awww. Do you like him?"

"I don't like him; I don't dislike him; but he sounds like he means business."

"Oh. My. God!" Nona replied.

"I know, right?"

"Well you've wanted this for a long time. Does it feel okay to you?"

"Yes. I'm petrified, but it feels good," Stephe answered. "I'ma do it."

"Well take care of yourself. I'd be petrified."

"I am!" Stephe agreed. "He has a lover, too."

"Wow. Be careful!"

Stephe was becoming thrilled at the idea, his hesitation vanishing. That night Stephe wrote Al an email:

"Hi, it's Stephe from Cliff's. Thanks for giving me your coordinates." He paused. What the hell was he going to write next? He sat staring at the screen for several minutes before taking the plunge. "I've never done anything like this before, but do you want to get together some time? –Stephe" and he hit "Send" before he could change his mind. He slammed the laptop shut and tossed it on the bed and went to the kitchen.

He'd become fairly adept at cooking for himself, since he was often home alone. He fried some hamburger meat, threw some Prego spaghetti sauce on it, and boiled some pasta in his mom's big pot. Fifteen minutes later he was enjoying his spaghetti at the kitchen table when his phone buzzed in his pocket.

An email. Al.

"Hey, no worries. It'd be great to see you. Name the time and place and we'll do it. - Al"

We'll do it. He said that on purpose.

Stephe could barely finish his spaghetti, suddenly not very hungry, his stomach in knots. He put the leftovers in the fridge, left the pot, pan and plate in the sink and hurried back up to his laptop.

He wrote Al back, and described his school and work schedule; Al wrote back and suggested this Sunday afternoon at his house on Douglass Street. "My lover is gone all week," he wrote. Ugh. Stephe had forgotten about that. The lover. In a way it excited him; it made it clandestine for the both of them.

The next day, Saturday, Al came into Cliff's twice getting supplies. The first time Stephe was busy cutting glass in the back and they could only smile and nod, but the second time, near closing, Al was back, getting some drywall screws.

"Hey." Stephe said, a stupid smile on his face, his cheeks burning red.

"Hey. I'm looking forward to tomorrow, wanna say two o'clock?"

"'Kay."

"Here's my address." Al wrote it on a slip of paper.

"'Kay," Stephe said again.

"Wear something casual," Al said, and, winking, walked up to the cash registers.

All that night Stephe was in a lather. Any hesitancy was gone, he was devoted to this new and frightening path. Tomorrow he was going to have sex for the first time.

He texted Nona.

"It's going to happen tomorrow at two."

"Are you scared?" she asked.

"Petrified."

"You'll do fine. Take pictures :-)"

"As if. What are you doing tomorrow?" he asked her.

"Well, I'm certainly not having sex," Nona replied. "I'll just be doing homework."

Sunday morning he could barely eat; he was so excited and nervous. But he fixed a big breakfast for Jack, Margery and himself, although he basically just pushed the food around on his plate with his fork. He tried to study but that was useless; he needed something to take his mind off what was going to happen at two o'clock.

Finally, at 1:45, he put on his jacket, told Marge he was going for a walk, and left.

Trudging up 18th Street to Douglass, Stephe felt like he was going to his own autopsy. He was petrified. Maybe this wasn't such a good idea after all. While his legs carried him forward, his mind stalled for ways to flake on Al without making him mad.

But he kept walking. Past the Edge Bar, Collingwood Street, onward he went as if to face his doom. He got to Douglass, turned left, went up the steps and rang the door buzzer. Heart in throat.

Al came to the door, wearing his usual jeans and white t-shirt.

"C'mon in," he said. "Nice to see you!"

Al grabbed Stephe's face with his hands and pulled him into a long, heart-stopping French kiss. Stephe marveled at the texture of Al's tongue. The piercing, the saliva. It lasted for several seconds as Al explored his mouth with his tongue, his goatee brushing Stephe's muzzle.

Finally they parted and walked from the open front doorway.

"Can I get you anything?" Al asked, leading Stephe into the hallway. His home was gorgeous, all very well done and tasteful.

"No thanks, I'm good," Stephe answered, following him into the house. Al took him straight back to his bedroom, a darkened room done in gray-blue walls with curtains drawn and a giant sleigh bed.

"Make yourself at home," Al answered and sat on the bed. He patted the bed next to him, an indication for Steve to come join him. Stephe did. He sat on the bed next to Al, remembering the same position with Henry, two years ago.

Two years! No wonder he was so horny.

No guessing this time as Al immediately began kissing him again on the bed. Stephe gave in to the momentum; he hugged Al and kissed him as he'd always imagined he would kiss a man, as he'd seen in all the movies; getting accustomed to the shock of Al's tongue and lips and facial hair. They leaned back on the bed in full embrace, making out, hugging and groping each other's bodies. Everything was for the first time. Stephe, fully committed to the situation, reached around and cupped Al's buttocks through his jeans, thrusting his hard on in his own Levi's into Al's. Al broke away and pulled off his shirt; Stephe did likewise.

Al stopped then, asking "Is this really your first time?"

Stephe nodded.

"I'm honored. I'm glad you're here! You tell me, then, what you want. Tell me what you've craved."

"Everything!" Stephe sighed breathlessly.

"Everything?" Al asked menacingly, wiggling his eyebrows.

"I think so." Stephe was nervous, not entirely sure he knew what "everything" meant to Al.

"Don't worry. You're in very good hands!" Al said warmly and kissed him again.

They continued, then; shirts off, hands on bodies, exploring, Stephe intrigued at touching so many tattoos and finding the skin surprisingly normal and warm. Al sucked Stephe's nipples, chewing on them so hard it hurt, and Stephe said "ow!"

"Sorry," Al responded and continued, softer this time, tonguing them briskly. It felt okay to Stephe. So he began chewing on Al's nipples which were much bigger and rougher, eraser-sized. Al seemed to like that, moaning his pleasure. Stephe bit them like Al had bitten him and Al shuddered in ecstasy.

Two men can do a lot with each other when suitably motivated. They left no stone unturned. All variations were tried; Stephe was free to explore another man's body as he'd ached to do all those years. They experienced each other to the fullest; Al was a very patient teacher. He seemed to know that Stephe would be on a hair trigger, likely to explode at the slightest touch. So he held him off for as long as he could before letting Stephe have the ball.

Suddenly it was done. Stephe was wrung out and jubilant. He did it!

He collapsed onto the bed and Al joined him. They kissed. "How'd I do?" Al asked.

"Oh, my God!" was all Stephe could say. "Oh, my God."

They embraced. Stephe felt sticky and warm and sweaty and cold, all at the same time.

"So that was really your first time?"

Stephe nodded.

"I'm glad. You did great! You think you're gonna like this?" Al asked, grinning.

"Hell, yeah!" Stephe replied.

"Good! We can do it more; as often as you like." Stephe was thrilled. He hugged Al again.

This wasn't the love affair he'd always wanted to have, but it was damn good. Damn good, indeed. Al looked very handsome to him all of a sudden.

But he wanted to go home. Wanted to tell Nona and Drew and everybody. Even Margery.

He looked at the clock and was shocked that it only said 2:35. It had felt like an eternity, but it had all taken place in half an hour.

"Lemme get ya a towel," said Al, jumping up from the bed and going into the bathroom. He brought back a hot wet towel, and Stephe sponged himself off. He went for his clothes and got dressed. Stephe was trembling like mad; weak in the knees.

"Do you want some water?" Al asked.

"Yes, please; that'd be great."

Al walked naked out of the room and Stephe looked at that beautiful butt, realizing all that he'd just been allowed to do, and his loins stirred again. But he was worn out. Al came back with a bottle of water from the fridge and Stephe gladly accepted it. His hands were trembling as he drank.

"Thank you again," Al said softly. "That was incredible!"

"Yeah. Thank you more!"

They stood and kissed and Al walked him, still naked, to the front door.

"I'll see you at work on Tuesday, I'm sure," Al promised.

"I'll be there," Stephe responded, and they pecked each other on the lips as Stephe went out the front door; it felt like being part of a couple and he was leaving to go to work in the morning. A peck on the lips.

"Bye," Al said.

"Bye," Stephe said, walking backwards down the front steps, looking at the naked man in the doorway. Finally he took his eyes away and headed back down Douglass Street to 18th.

He was on top of the world! Colors seemed brighter. The sunshine was wonderful. Birds were literally singing. He went to Starbucks at 18th and Castro, devastated that he didn't see anyone he knew but sat with his macchiato and texted Nona: "Oh my God!"

"Whaaaat?" she replied.

"It happened. Al. Just finished. It was INCREDIBLE!"

"Slut."

"I know!"

"Congratulations! How was it? I know, INCREDIBLE!"

"It was everything I'd ever dreamed, only better," he said.

"Good for you!"

"I feel warm all over and he says we can do it again. He was the perfect gentleman."

"You want that."

"I'm still trembling. Need nap," he said.

"You should do that. I have to head to work for a few hours,"

"'Kay."

"Congratulations! Bye!"

"TTYL <3" Stephe signed off.

Stephe finished his macchiato and went home and got into his own bed with his clothes on, but under the covers and curled up in a ball. He started to doze—caffeine be damned—recounting every step, every detail of what had just happened. As with his time with Henry, he wanted to remember it forever.

Chapter 5

With only thirty days left at high school, Stephe felt very grown up all of a sudden. It was hard to concentrate on his remaining month.

He'd taken his SAT exam earlier that spring and had done fairly well; it was a nerve-wracking week. His English scores were particularly high, but math not as good. He began the process of applying to University of California at Berkeley— his dream. Money wouldn't be a problem: His parents left their retirement accounts to Stephe and Jack with specific and generous provisions for education.

He spent a lot of time on the Berkeley admissions web page, following every step and working hard to make sure he didn't miss anything. He was determined.

He also applied to San Francisco State as a back-up, and, if everything failed, he was resigned to a year of community college if need be.

He continued to see Al about once a month— Al's lover (and now legally ex-husband) was never home, going on business trips or motorcycle runs as often as he could. Their lovemaking got better. But Stephe was never in love with Al; he was still looking for The One. Suddenly he found his fellow high schoolers not just uninteresting but truly rather pathetic. He viewed the older Castro residents around him with new eyes and an open heart.

He wanted love—true love. He didn't see himself as just another callous gay man.

At Cliff's a few weeks later Al was talking with some other guy and introduced him to Stephe as Marty. They chatted about this and that and when Marty walked away Al said "You should hook up with him. I had him over last week, and he's got an enormous dick!" Stephe was flabbergasted. Disgusted. He knew Al was in a relationship, but just how many men did he hook up with? He felt jealous. Of what, he couldn't say. But it left a sour taste in his mouth, just as he wondered just how big Marty's dick actually was. He was thrilled and disgusted all at the same time.

That was the crux of Stephe's problem. He didn't want to be a slut; he wanted romance with all the trimmings. He hated it when people spoke heartlessly about sex—it was too sacred. He was mad at Al for hooking up with Marty. He could tell his face had turned red. But he couldn't say what he was feeling to Al; he wouldn't understand.

Before he knew it, school was out and he was eighteen—and a free man. He graduated with a 3.8 GPA; Margery and Jack attended his graduation ceremony at the Cow Palace. He grabbed Nona in her cap and gown and they hugged and danced on the floor of the auditorium in joy.

He felt the loss of his parents keenly that day; wondered wistfully if they could be looking down to see him graduate, beaming with pride. But he just didn't believe in it.

Lilo the cat died in July. She'd become very thin and wouldn't eat. They took her to Mission Animal Hospital on Valencia just outside of the Burn Zone. She was diagnosed with tumors on her kidneys and the vet recommended she be put down.

"Lilo is on her last legs," the woman veterinarian said. "Her next step will be convulsions, and they could come at any time."

Stephe cried like a baby. Margery was there too, but remained stoic. Suddenly the loss of his parents came into it, too. Why did everyone have to die? Lilo was a link to his childhood, his life before the earthquake; happier times. He held Lilo as they gave her a tranquilizer. Her eyes rolled back in her head. Then came the hypodermic of pink goo, bringing the end. Stephe huffed and sniffled; Margery held herself coolly. Stephe knew that Margery saw death frequently at the hospital, so she had her reasons for remaining distant. But he wished she'd show even a modicum of sadness.

They made arrangements for cremation, paid the bill, and once they got back to the house, sans Lilo, Stephe found he had an email from Admissions at Berkeley: He was in!

He was sad and happy at the same time. A very bizarre combination of feelings. He called Nona.

"Wonderful news and horrible news," he said.

"Oh no. What's horrible?" she asked.

"Lilo just died; we had to put her to sleep just now."

"Aww, Stephe, I'm so sorry! She was such a sweetie."

"I know. I started thinking about the death of my parents and got very upset. It was ugly," Stephe admitted.

"Makes sense. I understand. The poor thing. I guess that just leaves Moana; does she even let you pet her?" Nona asked.

"Rarely. She's pretty uppity. Maybe now that Lilo's gone she'll come around; I don't know."

"What's your wonderful news?"

"I just got home to an email from Admissions at Berkeley. I'm in!"

"Oh my God, me too! I just found out." Nona shared the excitement.

They decided to go out to celebrate at Harvey's. They tried to order bloody marys, but were immediately carded.

Chapter 6

The United States in the year 2026 was a bleak place. Stephe and Nona were fairly insulated, living inside the liberal bubble of the Bay Area, but things were bad.

Donald Trump had served two terms as president, followed by former Florida Governor Rick Scott. The Supreme Court was stacked with hard-line conservatives following the death of Ruth Bader Ginsberg in 2021. Liberals were licking their wounds as environmental regulations were unspooled, education and transportation dismantled, and Welfare and Medicaid slashed across the board. Gay marriage was overturned, as was Roe vs. Wade and a myriad of union protections. True hunger and poverty returned to the United States in a way not seen since the 1930s. Shantytowns were everywhere. Homelessness, skyrocketing health care costs and a return of pre-existing conditions clauses became major concerns. The rich got richer and everyone else became much poorer.

Despite the improvements in the city's housing, the streets of San Francisco were littered with homeless people in a way that made the late 2010s seem quaint.

Crime and corruption were rampant. Donald Trump got his long-promised personal police force called The Freedom Fighters, a ragtag band of white supremacists, neo-Nazis and Proud Boys. They held rallies, bonked heads, and lynched blacks, gays and Muslims. Voter fraud became the norm. Mass shootings took place on a weekly basis.

In 2024, when Republican Rick Scott won the Office of the President, he had a solid Republican Senate and House of Representatives.

And thus the horrors of the Trump Administration continued. Hate crimes against minorities, Muslims, immigrants and gays reached a fever pitch: anti-gay legislation, under the guise of "religious freedom," sprang from state houses across the land, particularly in the South.

A great recession had struck in 2019, following the Trump trade wars.

By 2024 runaway inflation took the country in its grip. A one way BART ticket to Berkeley soared from $6.10 to $12 to $26 to $53 while Stephe was in school. Wages rose quickly to stop the gap, but that, in turn, just exacerbated the inflation.

California threatened to secede from the Union.

Chapter 7

First semester at Berkeley started at the end of August, 2026. Stephe wished he could experience living in a dorm on campus at Berkeley, but it just didn't make financial sense; he had a great big house almost to himself. Jack and Margery remained, Jack commuting to Stanford every day and working part-time as a paralegal, getting ready for his Bar Exam the following year. Margery had gained enough seniority that she didn't have to work the night shift at Davies Hospital as much anymore.

Even though times were tight, life continued apace at 472 Liberty Street. As a fortunate hedge against inflation, Stephen and Diana had a lot of their nest-egg in gold and utilities, so they were somewhat insulated against the steeply climbing prices.

Stephe kept his job at Cliff's until the store closed for good in December of 2026. Jobs were scarce, and Stephe needed his free time for studying, so he stayed unemployed, living off his inheritance while in school.

Jack found a girlfriend named Elena and they were getting pretty serious. Elena was a trim, elegant girl, a CPA, with black hair and dark brown eyes and, what Stephe assumed was an excellent figure. He liked her. Elena often slept over at the house; Stephe had a horror of having to hear muffled lovemaking from the bedroom across the hall.

As with any university, Stephe's class schedule was filled with "distribution requirements": various subjects not related to his projected major in English, but for which he needed credits. He wound up in Paleontology, Math 100—his math skills were still his weak point—and Native American History. While high school had been a cinch, he quickly learned that college was not—no handholding and no homework assignments that could be finished in ten minutes. He spent most of his time reading with a high-lighter in one hand, taking copious notes with the other.

The onrush of work was dizzying. Stephe took to the habit of studying in the Moffitt Library on campus or the Martin Luther King Student Union Building before heading home every night. He wanted to leave his school-work at school and not bring it home with him, but that dream quickly evaporated. He'd often work late into the night, trying to keep up. He was glad he didn't have a job to compete against his studying.

He usually met Nona for lunch; they didn't have any of the same classes that semester, but often carpooled together in Nona's car.

Every Tuesday night he went to the gay rap group off campus. Sometimes Eric the Hottie would be there, but he never showed any signs of interest in Stephe. He got to know some of the other attendees. No great love affairs reared their heads, but he became friends with André, a raucous and rather flaming African-American who always had stories to share of his large, loud family in Richmond, California, and his mother's refusal to accept him as gay.

"She still tries to fix me up with girls," he'd say. "I have more girlfriends than anyone I know; I usually wind up doing their hair and makeup." Everyone laughed.

The rap group was good therapy for Stephe. Nearly everyone in the group had lost loved ones in the earthquake; that was often the topic: So much grieving. The pain would feel as fresh to Stephe as the day he saw the ruins of Millennium Tower. It often became a crying jag with plenty of boxes of Kleenex on hand. It helped to get more of the tears out.

Just as often, though, talk would turn to the rapidly deteriorating quality of gay life in the United States. Forty-one states had eliminated—or never even had—laws on the books protecting the rights of lesbians, gays, bisexual or transgendered citizens. Stories were rampant of people losing jobs or apartments just for being gay or lesbian; life was becoming impossible in the deep south and many people migrated to the big cities in a way not seen since the 1970s.

Stephe finally found love in December, 2026. They met in Paleontology. It was a huge lecture hall, and he became aware of a bearded, stocky guy, about 220 pounds, with brown hair and brown eyes and a darling crease above his left eye. It gave a cute, quizzical look to his face. Adorable. Stephe would try to sit ever closer to him in class; then one day they wound up right next to each other. Desperate for something to say, Stephe resorted to the oldest trick in the book: He dropped his highlighter. The guy picked it up and their eyes met and they smiled.

"Thanks! How's it going?" Stephe asked nervously.

"Not so bad, thanks," the man answered. "I'm still not getting my head around the differences of the Cretaceous Period."

"I'm a Pleistocene man, myself," Stephe answered.

They chatted a bit about nothing; then the lecture began and they each turned to their respective laptops and worked through their notes. When the lecture was over, Stephe boldly asked the guy if he wanted to go get some coffee.

"Sure," was the welcome response.

Stephe followed him out of the lecture hall, acutely aware of the man's butt. They went to the 1951 Coffee Company in the Student Union Building and sat at a table with their lattes.

The man's name was Devin; he hoped to major in engineering. Devin did a lot of writing on the side, which was fascinating to Stephe, as he hoped to become a writer himself. They shared an interest in politics. Devin was from Aztec, New Mexico, in the Farmington area. He lived on campus in Blackwell Hall in a triple room; he was as jealous of Stephe having his own house in San Francisco as Stephe was jealous of Devin living in Blackwell Hall.

"Well, the grass is always greener," Devin said. "It's not easy living with two other guys in one room; there's absolutely no privacy. I can't even beat off unless I know they're asleep. Plus one of the guys in my unit, Tony, is completely gorgeous to me. I can't stand it!"

"And I'm sure he's straight, right?"

"As straight as they come."

"That's not fair!" Stephe laughed.

"Well, at least I get to see him naked."

They agreed to keep in touch, gave each other their phone number and email addresses, and sat next to each other in Paleontology class from then on.

They studied together—often at Blackwell Hall—so Stephe got to know some of the roommates. And he got to meet Tony. Devin was right: Tony was a god.

One cold sunny day, they had their first kiss in Sproul Plaza, aka Berkeley Central. They'd been talking on the bench and suddenly Devin leaned in and there it was and it happened.

They spent a lot of time together for about three weeks. Studying when they should, making out when they could. But it was a long time coming before they had the chance to make love.

It was on a rare day when Devin's roommates were all out. It was time, and Stephe was breathless.

They took their time, exploring each other's bodies, kissing and caressing. They passioned on each other. Devin was fuzzy in all the best places and they hungered for each other. It was glorious. Better than with Al—whom Stephe had not seen in quite a while. This time Stephe felt real love.

When they finished their first time at sex, spent as they were, they went out for ice cream, feeling all sticky and sweet. They talked for an hour before Stephe had to head for home in the dark winter night.

The first time Devin came across the bay and stayed the night with Stephe at 472 Liberty Street was a dream come true. Stephe had never had the joy of sleeping next to a man, and he found it good and he found it warm—even in Stephe's tiny full-sized bed. Devin had a light snore that Stephe found charming; he loved the way Devin would sort of kick his feet as he fell asleep.

Margery was home when he brought Devin in; he introduced them to each other and simply said that Devin was staying the night. Margery said nothing.

One day about a week later Stephe went into Blackwell Hall to see Devin. The building doors were always locked but someone was usually coming or going, so he got himself inside and he took the stairs up. He walked through the common room, smelling the smells of a dormitory; antiperspirant and feet and dirty underwear. He knocked on Devin's door and Devin answered, hiding himself behind the door, obviously naked.

"Hey. You okay?" Stephe asked.

"Yeah, just . . . uh . . . studying," Devin answered, still hiding himself behind the door, acting tense.

"Okay. Well. If you're busy," Stephe offered.

"Sorry, yeah, I kinda am,"

By now Stephe had his hackles up and a sick feeling in the pit of his stomach. His bowels felt like they were going to drop. His face felt flushed.

"Well, I'll leave you to it See you in class tomorrow?"

"Um, yeah, sure."

"Okay. See ya." Stephe said, wondering if he'd ever see the damn man again in his life. He turned and left, his heart sinking and his face red.

He walked in a daze. He started to get angry. Very angry. And hurt. Devin obviously had a guy in there, there was no other explanation. He even wondered, foolishly, if it was Tony.

He argued both sides with himself; Devin was his first real boyfriend, and Stephe had hopes for it. Should he still continue to see him? Could he do it? He was too damn mad right now. It wasn't what he'd had in mind. He wanted to cast Devin out; he was the villain, he broke the rules.

Rules? What "rules"? They hadn't set any rules, it simply hadn't come up.

Well, it was up now. And Stephe felt like he wasn't going to stand for it. He'd rather be alone again than just part of Devin's ensemble cast.

He had reading to do, but he knew that was going to be impossible, so, blowing off his homework, he went home with Nona at her normal time of 6:00 p.m.

Traffic was a nightmare at the MacArthur Maze and the Bay Bridge toll plaza.

Stephe told Nona what had just happened. He was sick to his stomach as they nosed their way through the traffic.

"I felt like an idiot standing there."

"Aw, Honey, I'm so sorry!" Nona replied.

"Me too. I keep wondering if I'm doing the right thing. By walking away, I mean."

"I know most gay relationships are open, but this is too much," Nona said. "You guys were just starting to date. Most people, if they're serious, would lighten up on extracurricular activities for a while."

"That's what I keep coming back to," Stephe said, thankful that his friend understood. "I obviously didn't mean as much to him as I thought."

"So you have to decide: Take him back or tell him to go to hell."

"I want to be able to be cool about it, but I'm so not. I'm too damn mad!"

"Well there's your answer," Nona said.

"I wonder if I'll ever be cool about being in an open relationship. I know that's the norm for gay men, but I just can't picture it," Stephe admitted.

"Well, today you can't. That's okay. Cut yourself some slack. You've just suffered your first real defeat. There will be other guys; maybe find one that isn't such a turd."

Things at the house seemed dark and lifeless. Moana came in and cuddled with him, something she never did.

He just kept picturing it, some guy in there having sex with Devin. It infuriated him; made him sick to his stomach. He felt humiliated.

Next day in Paleontology class Stephe sat somewhere else, with no open seats around him. But soon, to his horror, the girl next to him got up to sit with a friend and, before he had time to register, Devin plopped down into the empty chair. Stephe was aghast. He didn't know what to say. His heart was in his throat.

"Sorry about last night," Devin said cautiously.

"It's cool; we never said we were exclusive."

Despite his embarrassment, Stephe was determined to play it breezy in front of Devin. He wrapped himself in his shame and hatred—it felt familiar to him, like an old blanket. He chose to feel the hurt.

At the end of class he gathered his laptop and left without saying goodbye to Devin. He didn't even look back.

Chapter 8

He didn't try to have any boyfriends for a while after that. He felt dirty. He got his Spring schedule and diligently studied his new subjects, still struggling with math. He took on a tutor to help, a German guy named Armin. Armin helped somewhat.

On Sunday, June 7, 2026, neo-Nazis held a surprise rally in Sproul Plaza.

"We gotta go," said Nona.

"Yeah. We do," Stephe agreed.

Stephe and Nona shared a hastily made sign—"Back into the closet, Fucking Nazis!"—and there were hundreds of protesters on the south end of the plaza. A few Berkeley Campus Police in riot gear were in the middle and, behind them, the Berkeley Police. To the north were Proud Boys, neo-Nazis and white supremacists. Chants and screams . . the groups converged with the police in the middle. Stephe and Nona were in the front. It quickly turned into a mêlée, shoving and kicking, and the cops tried more to get out of the way than to help.

Stephe couldn't help but notice how good-looking some of the neo-Nazis were.

But that quickly ended when he got truncheoned by a sign reading something with the word "Fags" on it. It became a battle, swings and punches and kicks. Stephe got kicked in the belly and went "Whoof!" He doubled over and was king hit on the way down. Nona was over him, trying to protect him from the stomping feet. Rather than the helpless feeling he had that night in Dolores Park so long ago, this time he was mad. He made his way to his feet again and punched a neo-Nazi in the jaw, remembering to follow through with the jab as he'd heard them say on TV. His hand hurt! But the neo-Nazi went down with his own "Whoof!" and Stephe, pissed by this time, stomped on him with his Adidas shoe.

The police had grown in number and started pushing in from the East, spraying tear gas as they came. Several people fell then, hands over their faces and their stinging eyes. Instantly, cartons of milk were passed up from behind, to pour over the first victims' eyes and noses to reduce the stinging of the gas.

The police then charged in, batons swinging, hitting people on both sides of the fight indiscriminately. Nona got cracked on the head; Stephe, his hands out to protect her, got his knuckles rapped so hard by a baton he feared his hand was broken.

It was a free-for-all. Students were beating police, police were beating students. neo-Nazis were beating police, police were beating neo-Nazis, everyone continued beating each other and kicking.

Finally, the riot police had grown in numbers to the point where they started dragging protestors away, two cops per student, handcuffing them and throwing them to the ground face first. Handcuffed bodies began to pile up, mostly students and very few neo-Nazis.

Stephe and Nona were thus treated, yanked from the confusion, handcuffed and thrown onto the kicking, squirming pile.

"Why are you arresting *us!?*" Nona kept screaming.

Over a hundred student protesters were arrested and only thirteen Proud Boys. They were dragged to vans and driven to the police department on Martin Luther King Jr. Way, tears streaming from their eyes and snot flowing freely—no way to wipe your nose when you're handcuffed—and held for four hours and charged with disturbing the peace. A misdemeanor. No bail was set.

"This is goddamned bullshit!" Nona kept repeating. They weren't released until after 7:30 p.m. They were starving. Despite Stephe's hand being possibly broken, they grabbed a bite to eat on Telegraph Avenue before Stephe decided he should go to the Emergency Room at Alta Bates to have his hand looked at. Nona said she'd go, too; she had quite a crack on the head from the police baton.

The ER was a mad house. Dozens of people with riot injuries lined the hallways, spilling out of the waiting room.

"Fuck this," said Nona. "I don't think I have a concussion. Do you want to stay?"

"I don't. I'll have Margery look at my hand at home; it'll be much quieter at Davies Hospital if she thinks I should go in."

"Okay, let's blow this cluster fuck," Nona said. "Ride with me back into town?"

"Sure. Thanks."

They walked to Nona's 2020 Nissan Sentra, and she drove out to the 80 Freeway.

"You sure you're good to drive? I don't want you to have a brain hemorrhage. You could kill us all," joked Stephe.

"Naw, I'm good. I read that if you have a concussion you see double. I just have a gash and a bump."

The Bay Bridge Toll Plaza was backed up some, but they nosed their way through the FasTrak lane and headed up the lacy eastern span.

Through the tunnel at Yerba Buena Island, on the old traditional Bay Bridge span, the view of the city was incredible. Stephe would always marvel at the beauty of San Francisco; many construction cranes still littered the skyline, forever building after the earthquake.

He missed the sight of the huge lumbering Sutro TV Tower, taken down in 2023. It was an ugly thing, but you always knew where you were in relation to it.

"So come to my house and have Margery look you over," he suggested.

"Okay, hopefully, if I can find a place to park."

She did, a few doors down on Liberty Street, and they went in to 472 to find Margery on the couch in the living room, watching Fox News, her arms crossed. They were showing drone footage of the riots and decrying the arrest of innocent Freedom Fighters, cheering the fact that hundreds of student protestors had been arrested and taken into custody.

"Hi Marge," Stephe said, indicating the TV. "We were just there and got a little banged up. I was wondering if you could take a look? The ER at Alta Bates was a mob scene so we didn't stay."

"I might have known you'd be there," Margery said snappishly. "Let's see what you have."

"You go first," Stephe offered Nona and led her to Margery; she sat next to her on the sofa.

"I got beaned on the head by a police baton," Nona explained. She bent her head toward Margery; the latter grabbed her head and traced the bump with her finger. Nona winced.

"Well, it didn't break the skin, which is good; it would have bled like mad. Any dizziness or blurred vision?"

"No, it just hurts like hell," Nona replied.

"I bet it does! Since your vision is normal and you're not dizzy I doubt it's a concussion. Still, keep a watch for vision problems, and I'd ice it if I were you," Margery advised.

"I will. Thanks!" Nona got up and gestured to Stephe to have a seat next to Margery.

"There's an ice pack in the freezer," Margery continued. "Go ahead and grab it and start icing while I take a look at Stephe."

Stephe sat down and showed Margery his badly swollen left hand.

"Oh, dear, this one's much worse," Margery said. "Can you wiggle your fingers?"

"Not really; I haven't attempted to."

"Do it now, please," Margery encouraged.

Stephe tried; he experienced great pain. The fingers wouldn't budge.

"You've got broken fingers, looks like," she said. "We should take you to Davies for X-rays."

"Wow. It sure hurts," moaned Stephe.

"Do you want me to go with you?" asked Nona, fresh from the kitchen holding an ice pack to her head.

"Naw. It'll be boring. I'll just go and get some reading done while I'm there."

"Want me to go?" asked Margery.

"No, thanks, Marge. You get enough of that place; you deserve a day off. I'm glad you were home though."

"Okay, I'll call you an Uber."

"Oh, that's fine Ms. Johnson, I can drop Stephe off in my car. I might as well get home and rest. Or study, if I can."

"That would be great. Feel free to keep the ice pack."

"Thank you, and thanks for examining us."

"My pleasure. Take care." And she turned back to

Fox News announcing new cuts to the EPA by the Scott Administration and what a boon it would be to the beleaguered economy.

"Let's go," said Nona.

"I gotta pee first," Stephe said.

"Okay," Nona answered.

He went and did that, not washing his solitary functioning hand.

Nona dropped him off at Davies up the road. "You missed it. Fox News was talking about shooting more migrants crossing the Mexican border like it was a positive thing, and your aunt was just lapping it up."

"Yep. That's Marge. It's sad, really, I don't know how she can stand living in an area where nobody thinks like she does; no wonder she turns to Faux News to keep her company."

"We just left a couple of hundred neo-Nazis on Sproul Plaza; your aunt can always hook up with them when she gets lonely."

"Gross," Stephe said.

"Well, here we are; get that hand taken care of," Nona instructed him.

"I will. Thanks for the ride."

"Thanks for taking a baton to the hand. That one was directed at my head!" Nona said.

They kissed each other on the cheek and Stephe climbed out of the Sentra and headed into the ER.

Palacio was still working the desk. She didn't remember Stephe, but he remembered her from the night he got queerbashed two years ago. She had him sign some forms, took his insurance card and told him to wait.

It was a couple of hours before Stephe was seen by a nurse practitioner. He tried to read *Moll Flanders*.

X-rays were taken; he had three broken fingers, and they had to be reset. They numbed up his hand the best they could and proceeded to pull on each finger, making sure they each set in the right way. Stephe yelped loudly. The local anesthesia they gave him was not strong enough to hide the whole pain, but it helped. They put his hand in a brace and wrapped it up and sent him home with Ibuprofen.

"Can I get Vicodin? It really hurts."

"We're not allowed to give out Vicodin anymore. New drug laws; you know," the doctor responded.

Yeah, Stephe knew. But it was worth a shot.

He decided to walk home, it wasn't that far and it was a nice night for it. By then it was nearly eleven o'clock. He wished he was old enough to go into a bar. If anything called for a drink this did. But he was only nineteen. Two years to go.

Doing schoolwork was difficult with just one hand, but Stephe soldiered on; he got through *Moll Flanders* and laboriously wrote his report, pecking with one hand on the keyboard. Only got a 3.3 on his paper, but seriously didn't remember much about the book except how many times she got married. It was all a blur.

Chapter 9

In 2028 Apple released the Muon™: the size of a grain of rice, this tiny device, inserted beneath the skin in your left wrist, served as cell-phone, internet, bank account and credit card. It changed everything. Toll roads, Customs and Immigration, even voting was done by Muon. People still needed screens, which were lightweight fold-ups in your pocket, a cross between an iPhone and iPad with cameras, microphones, and keyboards. But every bit of data was stored in the Muon. Buying groceries? Just swipe your wrist over the sensor. Getting on BART? Swipe your wrist.

Some people decried the technology, claiming it to be the biblically prophesied mark of the Beast.

But the Muon quickly became indispensable.

Stephe got one fairly soon after they came out, intrigued by the technology. At first they didn't do much; not many places accepted them for payment. But within two years, cash was obsolete. Every business took Muon payments.

Various hacks became available; one was called *Click!* If you were sexually interested in someone it would detect your hormones and heart rate and send a click signal to the other person's Muon. It was fun at parties. Stephe downloaded the hack and set it to male-only.

The first time he got a Muon *Click!* he was at a party in a house in Berkeley with Nona and André. He was having a boring evening, so he was charmed when his Muon *Click!*ed; yet a mousy man named Guy came over and introduced himself and started talking to him. Stephe wasn't interested, but was as gracious as he could be. He thanked Guy for the *Click!* He managed to extricate himself, hopefully with no feelings hurt.

Stephe continued at Berkeley, knocking out his distribution requirements and finally getting English classes. He hooked up a few times with a few guys; his first mutual Muon *Click!* happened in the coffee shop, with a guy named Norman. They had it off a few times but their personalities didn't mesh well at all. No one moved Stephe toward love, but he enjoyed his occasional forays into sex. A few regulars. Continued commuting from 472 Liberty Street.

Jack had passed his bar exam in 2026 and was junior man at a law firm in downtown San Francisco.

Margery was still Margery.

Chapter 10

Stephe quickly learned to his chagrin that majoring in English was a snooze fest. Literature classes were the mainstay of the major. You read books by the dozen: *Moby Dick, Sense and Sensibility, Vanity Fair, Catch 22*—the list was endless. And you had to write reports on them. How can you write about something so boring without using Google? Nothing you could say wouldn't have been said millions of times many years ago by people far smarter than you.

If there was anything worse than being a student of literature, Stephe imagined it would have to be being an English Lit professor, needing to read all that dross, year after year.

He became discouraged. But it was in his creative writing classes that Stephe found his passion. He loved it. He had a hard time finding plots for stories; they just wouldn't come. He found he could describe a character, set a mood, set a feeling and set the whole thing up; he just couldn't make his characters *do* anything. It was frustrating in the extreme.

He focused on his journalism courses and found he was best at personal essay writing.

In March of 2029, his third year at Berkeley, Stephe was awarded a coveted internship at *The Daily Californian*, the Berkeley newspaper.

He was in heaven! He decided to tweak his major and go into journalism. It meant a few extra semesters, since his focus had been English Lit, but he was on fire.

The Daily Californian still published a handful of paper copies distributed all over campus every morning, but mostly it was read online. It was his golden opportunity to move ahead with his new degree in Journalism. *The Daily Californian* was a serious news organization, not just for the school itself but for the surrounding areas as well, covering Berkeley city politics and the police force. He started small, helping, at first, with the classified ads and events calendars, but he got to know the inner workings of the place. Soon he was writing copy for small stories and working with the bloggers and reporters. He was fascinated with web design and jealous of the IT guys so he took a few classes in HTML and CSS. He got so he could do some edits to the main web page and have them come out okay.

But his main focus was on writing.

He published articles about racism within the Berkeley police department, with tons of statistics to back it up. He got the inside scoop on Berkeley City Hall and became a regular fixture at city meetings. He got to know the inner workings of a news team. His writing improved.

It wasn't long before he met a guy. Taylor Baldwin. Taylor was a daily blogger; he didn't often show up at *The Daily Californian* in person, but when he did he certainly caught Stephe's attention. Ginger, ginger beard—heaven for Stephe—and freckles that (Stephe was thrilled to eventually learn) covered his body entirely except for the soles of his feet. A bit too slender for Stephe's liking, but sometimes that boded well for other things, like personal endowment.

Their Muons *Click!*ed. They managed to strike up a

conversation and it went well. They wound up having dinner, and once again Stephe became excited about a man. Their viewpoints clashed; Taylor was a little high-strung, always blurting out what he thought and having an argument for everything. Still, they'd hold hands and kiss and it was good.

Taylor had roommates that were always there, so they hadn't had the chance to consummate their relationship for two agonizing weeks. One night Stephe was finally free and clear to ask Taylor over to 472 Liberty Street so they could have some privacy. Jack and Margery were out.

When they came out of the Muni Underground at Castro Station, the air was bitterly chilled from the fog, a good fifteen degrees cooler than Berkeley just across the bay. Taylor didn't have a jacket so Stephe lent him his. They decided to have a drink at Twin Peaks—it was just a month after Stephe's twenty-first birthday and he was pleased he wasn't carded; having facial hair evidently helped. After their drinks they walked the east side of the street along the Castro Theatre and he showed Taylor the site of the old Cliff's Hardware store, now a Baby Gap™ store.

Once at the house they went to Stephe's old room and kissed each other in the darkness, with just a solitary lamp over the desk on. (It was incandescent. Stephe despised compact flourescents and the light they gave out. He had ordered traditional Edison bulbs from Amazon to enjoy much warmer light).

They unwrapped each other in the warm light and Stephe was delighted and amazed at Taylor's aquiline beauty. So slender and toned! His suspicions on Taylor's endowment were right.

"You know what we call these," he said, grabbing Taylor's erection.

"What?"

"Blue points!" he said rubbing the bluish head of Taylor's erect member with his thumb. "Only redheads get them, that's why we call you guys blue points."

They laughed. They made love. Taylor stayed the night. It was a Friday, so no need to wake up early the next morning. They talked and slept in the full-sized bed, huddled together for warmth as it was a chilly night and the heat wasn't on.

Mid-morning they awoke, and Stephe brought Taylor coffee in bed. Margery was in the kitchen, just off the night shift and they exchanged pleasantries; Stephe took two cups of coffee up to his room and Margery said nothing.

Stephe and Taylor had a wondrous affair for three months. They were walking on air.

But it had a time limit. Taylor was to graduate in June and had already laid plans to move to New York when his time at Berkeley ended. He made no secret of it.

The two men loved each other and enjoyed the three months they had. It was the closest Stephe had gotten to a real boyfriend, although they rarely had the occasion for a tumble.

But Taylor moved away.

It was hard on Stephe. They shared a tearful goodbye, and then that was it. They promised to keep in touch, but it soon fell to bits as Taylor had a new city to learn and all new people to meet.

After Taylor left Stephe saw a few guys here and there; even found that he liked three-ways when he briefly dated a couple of guys off College Avenue. The possibilities were endless. He marveled that the two men, Tony and Mark, weren't possessive of each other in the slightest. They'd even let him spend the night, all three of them cozy in bed. Stephe learned how sleeping between two men leaves you dangerously overheated under the covers. But he liked it immensely.

Nona began seeing an artist named Joe; a tall, dark and quiet brooding man. Although they weren't ready to move in together yet, Nona decided to move out of the apartment on 16th Street with her father and live in Berkeley.

"It's just time," she said. "My father and I haven't ever really gotten along, particularly after losing Mom in the earthquake. In a way I feel guilty leaving Dad to stew in his own juices, but it'll do me good to get away. I'm very excited to be moving to Berkeley. I can't really afford it unless I sell my car, but I won't really need it anymore."

"Do you have a place picked out?" Stephe inquired.

"I've narrowed it down to two," Nona answered. "They're both nice; they're both slightly out of my price range. I have to pick the one with the best roommate."

"Well, after your father, a roommate should be a piece of cake."

"Tell me about it! I think I like the one on Shattuck best; ground floor with a little garden and a couple of cats. The roommate *seems* normal. Girl named Natalie."

"Don't they always, at first?" Stephe agreed.

"Yeah. I don't think she's a bunny-boiler or anything, but she might be a little uptight. The place is spotlessly clean, and I have a rather nonchalant approach to housekeeping."

"You and me both."

"I think I'll go for it. I only hope she isn't too anal," she said.

"You gonna call her?" Stephe asked.

"Yeah," Nona said. "I'm going for it."

Nona called Natalie and took the room.

Stephe helped her move out, making many trips across the Bay Bridge. Nona's father Francisco was sullen at her moving out. He didn't say much, just drank beer in front of the television.

Natalie wound up being pretty cool after all. Yes, she was anal; everything had to be just so. But Nona got into the swing of things and she and Natalie became pretty good friends.

They got into the habit, every Thursday night—Stephe, Nona and Natalie—of having spicy chicken at Mom's Teriyaki on Shattuck Avenue. Sometimes André from the rap group would join them when he could. Such a simple ritual, but the food and company were always good and it was warm and nice.

Jack, still dating Elena, moved in with her in Bernal Heights, leaving Stephe alone with Margery in the house.

Moana, the Siamese cat, finally died. They decided not to get any more cats since no one was ever there to enjoy their company.

Chapter 11

Stephe graduated in the spring of 2031, two semesters late, having tweaked his major late in the game. So he missed out on the June graduation ceremony and all the pomp and circumstance. He just finished his last exam and—that was it. He quietly walked off campus a free man. As a graduate, his time at *The Daily Californian* was over.

It was like an explosive decompression. He went from a hundred miles an hour to zero, full-stop. Hanging around 472 Liberty Street, he was unemployed and had to remind himself to take a shower every day. He began playing around with Al again. By that time they were like old lovers.

With their parent's room unoccupied, and, with permission from Margery, Stephe turned the master bedroom into his own room. He totally redecorated it. He was tired of living in the same room his whole life, filled with adolescent belongings; he wanted a fresh start. He painted the room with cool colors and bought nice furniture and art. He didn't know what to do about the bed—his parents' bed. It was a nice pillow top mattress in fine condition, and a knotty pine four-poster frame. He decided to keep it. It was a connection to his parents and it made him feel good. He was probably conceived in that self-same four-poster bed.

Nona got hired by an advertising company in North Park and Stephe was glad for her; but she worked long hours and didn't have much time for him.

He needed to get a job.

He tried all the major Bay Area news organizations first; he had a few promising interviews, one at the *San Francisco Chronicle* and another at KTVU Channel Two news. But they didn't pan out. He set his sights lower, applied to the *San Francisco Bay Guardian, The Bay Area Reporter,* and even the old *San Francisco Examiner.*

He finally landed a job as a copy editor for a tech magazine in a small publishing house south of Market—very boring stuff and not well paid. The subject matter was of little interest to him. They published news and blogs related to the tech world; Stephe could barely wrap his head around it. He only worked there six months.

He kept his feelers out and eventually got hired by the Gay Liberation Front.

The original Gay Liberation Front had been a small group started in New York in 1969 following the Stonewall Riots. It was a pretty extreme, fringe political group. That project was abandoned in 1972.

The banner of the Gay Liberation Front was taken back up again in San Francisco in 2023 after the dissolution of gay marriage and several states' revocation of gay rights. A political lobby headquartered on Harrison Street, the GLF's main mission was support, counseling, legal help and political promotion. Taking a page from the old Act Up movement, the GLF was a strident, in-your-face advocacy group. They organized sit ins, marches, and demonstrations. They put stickers all over town.

An entire branch of the GLF was devoted to documentation and archiving the history of gay persecution. Since no one else was doing it, the Gay Liberation Front started a nationwide database of gay rights violations, and had thousands of on-camera interviews with survivors of gay violence, cross-referenced. They even had interactive 3-D videos where you could ask questions and find answers.

The offices of the GLF were in the Mission in a rebuilt masonry building on Harrison Street, an easy commute for Stephe on the 33 Stanyan bus line.

The GLF became of nationwide importance with chapters across the country. It was well-funded. An entire legal team was at their disposal. Lawyers—including many famous and high profile attorneys—donated their time to lend aid to gay and lesbian causes. The organization developed sizable political pull. They had the eyes and ears of all liberal senators and representatives, and they became a force to be reckoned with.

Stephe was hired as a reporter for their weekly journal, *Equality*. As such, he became an expert. He reported on gay bashings and rights violations from his seat in the news division. He got a front row view of the horrors unfolding across America as the tide against lesbians and gays rolled back into uncharted territory.

He became polarized and somewhat famous.

The office was a dynamic place to work—extremely hectic and reactionary. His boss, David, was a very difficult man, very hands on; he edited Stephe's copy without mercy. Stephe knew David was shaping him into being the best writer he could be, but it was hard to not hold a grudge. He and David did not like each other in the slightest. They forged a respectable working relationship, but beneath the surface Stephe often seethed.

His closest co-worker, the web designer, was Craig. He was super hot to Stephe. It was sweet agony to work in such close proximity. Craig was straight; married, with a kid named Joel. Stephe's Muon *Click!*ed like mad, to no avail. Stephe loved it and hated it, all at the same time.

Nicole was his favorite at the office. Stephe fell in "like" with her the minute he saw her. Nicole was a tall buxom blonde who used to be a man named Robert. She was the office manager and in charge of payroll. She was bright and funny, and she was very open about her transition. You could ask her anything. She began her transformation in 2028, starting with hormones and cross-dressing; then came the breast augmentation and a facelift. Nicole was often mistaken for a hot woman—she even had a few suitors. The UPS guy flirted with her endlessly and she loved it.

The work was stimulating but horrifying. Stephe had to report it all: Gay life in America was coming apart at the seams.

It began incrementally, as all such things do: revocation of gay rights, and then Facebook banning any discussion of gayness—flagging it as "inappropriate" under the guise of protecting children. Fewer and fewer outlets existed for being openly gay, particularly in the red states.

The gay porn industry was starved into non-existence by a series of laws—again, under the pretext of protecting children. Gay dating apps like Grindr, Scruff and Growlr weren't banned outright, but they became dangerous places with neo-Nazis impersonating gay men on the make. They'd lure an unsuspecting victim into an apartment only to find a mob waiting for them. They'd be tortured and beaten and the whole thing uploaded to YouTube. Sometimes the victims' fingers would be cut off.

Gay bumper stickers had all but vanished as people who weren't lucky enough to live in big cities went back into the closet. Small-town gay bars began closing.

At its height, America had twenty states with laws on the books to protect gay rights. By 2031 only two still had them: New York and California. A few lynchings had taken place; beatings were commonplace. Kids were being kicked out of their homes when their parents discovered they were gay or lesbian. Conversion therapies were on the rise where previously they had been banned as inhumane.

Gay agencies—and even other chapters of the GLF in other cities—were being firebombed on a regular basis.

It all pressed down on Stephe. He became the go-to person in the country for gay rights violations. His email inbox was rarely below ten thousand emails. He heard cries for help out in the darkness.

He couldn't sleep at night under the onslaught.

Chapter 12

Scandal rocked the already neurotic nation in the 2030 U.S. midterms on Tuesday, November 5th. Half the people voted by Muon. The election was blithely, ridiculously hacked.

What was predicted to be an easy landslide by the Democrats turned into an embarrassing Republican victory. It was a rout.

Liberals took to the streets by the tens of thousands. A general strike was declared and the country shut down.

Republican President Mitch Kellum, elected in 2028, urged calm, but the damage was done. Calls for the election to be overturned sprang from all parts of the country. Kellum denied any wrongdoing. It was the Russians and the Chinese, he claimed, determined to destabilize the U.S.

Democrats had lost all remaining political power and the conservative U.S. Supreme Court upheld the election in predictable fashion, six to three.

It was like a bomb had gone off. Protests turned to riots. Far-right fundamentalists took to the streets in support of the election, and faced off with teeming hordes of furious liberals. A nation that had been savagely divided, blue against red, liberal against conservative for the past thirteen years, would eventually fall into violence. It finally happened in Philadelphia on November 9, 2030. Rioting liberals clashed with Freedom Fighters, neo-Nazis, and

Proud Boys on Market Street at the beautiful Philadelphia City Hall building. Fisticuffs, brawls, burning cars. Shots rang out. The police, caught in the middle, fell apart; each officer defected to his or her side of the political divide and joined the fight.

The Culture War had begun.

Battlements were hastily built in the streets of Washington, DC, New York, Chicago, Seattle, Los Angeles, Miami, Atlanta, and Minneapolis. It was bedlam. The streets became littered with bodies as street fights broke out: Red versus Blue, Conservative versus Liberal.

People fled the cities only to find skirmishes in the suburbs. Ikea parking lots were battle zones. A Home Depot in Enid, Oklahoma, was burnt to the ground. Fires started everywhere.

The country spasmed in violence, hand to hand, block by block. After thirteen years of political loggerheads, the center could no longer hold. Any attempt at civil discourse fell on deaf ears. It was us against them, everywhere.

A typical confrontation would be as follows: Unarmed Liberals vastly outnumbered armed Freedom Fighters. They'd go toe-to-toe in the streets, yelling and waving signs in confrontation. Fist fights would break out. But then someone would get mad, grab their gun, and start shooting. Others would join in and the unarmed protesters would flee back behind barricades of cars, buses, dumpsters and buildings, leaving the dead and wounded in the street. It was like a form of trench warfare—and this was played out in cities and towns across the country. Attack and retreat. Attack and retreat. And anger—people were incredibly angry. They fought tooth and nail, neighbor against neighbor, family member against family member.

In San Francisco the tens of thousands of liberals lining Market Street day after day eventually found themselves being bludgeoned by Freedom Fighters. Skirmish lines fell into place along the main street and shots were fired. Freedom Fighters were hopelessly outnumbered though and, despite having guns, were quickly overpowered by the throngs of San Franciscans. They fled.

Stephe was there with Nicole. They'd come up from Harrison Street to take part in the demonstration that day. Nicole wound up hitting a neo-Nazi with her shoe, bloodying his face while Stephe—feeling nothing but cold rage—just took his rifle and hit him with it.

The National Guard had to be mobilized to quell the riots, and still it wasn't enough. The U.S. Army and the Marines were added and took to the streets with water cannons and tear gas.

Finally the main fights in the bigger cities were quelled by force. After six bloody days the spasm ended. Thousands were dead. Many more thousands were arrested by the military and taken to separate camps, red and blue, for disturbing the peace and inciting violence.

Thus began a new Cold War as Americans could no longer speak to one another.

The Republican regime wasted no time enacting its most draconian measures yet. Quality of life deteriorated in the U.S. sharply. After eight years of Trump and four of Rick Scott, America finally got its *Atlas Shrugged* moment. Grover Norquist famously said in 2001, "I don't want to abolish government. I simply want to reduce it to the size where I can drag it into the bathroom and drown it in the tub." He got his wish. Environmental legislation was a thing of the past. Social Security was bankrupt, as was Medicare. Healthcare had been dismantled by the courts. Civil rights: Gone. Gay rights: Gone. Restaurants, colleges and businesses of all sorts could legally refuse to serve African-Americans, Muslims, gays, Jews, liberals and immigrants. Labor unions had been starved and broken. NASA and the U.S. Postal Service were privatized.

Huge corporations ruled the dying land. Everyone was poor but the stock market continued to soar. CEO pay was now 2200% that of the average worker. Inflation had somehow stabilized from the early 2020s but housing prices steadily climbed. No one could afford rent.

Stephe, in his capacity at the Gay Liberation Front, got first-hand views of the lives of his fellow Americans: starvation wages, toxic drinking water, corrupt police, beatings, lynchings, food riots, and bread lines.

Climate change continued to wreak havoc: Summers were hotter, winters were colder and, since government subsidies for heating and cooling were gone, people froze to death in their own homes. Air quality deteriorated. Drinking water became scarce as industrial pollution spread unchecked.

Supersonic jets once again came into service, cutting travel times by two-thirds but re-polluting the stratosphere and rending the air with sonic booms. Money was out there to be made, the environment be damned.

The poles were melting at an increasing rate, threatening South Florida with inundation. A Dust Bowl occurred in 2030, decimating agriculture in the heartland. Hurricanes, droughts, floods and fires increased each year. And in the middle of it all sat the Freedom Fighters and Evangelical Republicans basking in what they called the End Times.

Things weren't just bad in the U.S. Europe had fallen apart, too. Muslim extremists enacted constant terror bombings. Individual European borders were put back in place. The European Union was disbanded and fighting had broken out between Germany and Poland, and between post-Brexit Great Britain and France.

India, Russia and China dominated the world stage. With strong totalitarian governments and big budgets, they hogged all the world's resources, while the United States quietly fell apart.

A Great Depression struck in 2031. The Stock Market lost 70% of it's value on Black Friday, August 29th. World markets started to collapse. Unemployment skyrocketed to 30%. More bread lines and shanty towns. Hyper-inflation once again took hold. People were glued to their screens, watching as their savings and retirement accounts were wiped out. Bank of America and Chase Bank collapsed. General Motors shut down.

Then the bombings began. Churches, schools, liberal organizations like the NAACP and Planned Parenthood, gay organization headquarters. It became a nearly daily occurrence.

In December, 2031, Three Mile Island, the beleaguered nuclear reactor of fame, was sabotaged and melted down. The entire area had to be evacuated and would be for the foreseeable future. Hershey and Harrisburg, Pennsylvania, became ghost towns.

Each side blamed the other, but it wasn't hard to tell who had all the guns, ammo and explosives at their disposal. Proud Boys, Freedom Fighters and Alt-Right Coalitions began boldly taking the credit for the bombings and sabotage. The FBI and CIA, hamstrung by the Kellum Administration, did little to curb the violence.

Chapter 13

Life in San Francisco was grim, but people soldiered on. Renewed calls came for California to secede from the United States, and this time it started gaining serious traction.

For Stephe the biggest problem was Margery. He knew she was in the minority in San Francisco. Margery, a solid red Republican, lived in the gayest neighborhood in the most liberal state in the Union. He didn't know how to talk to her. She quietly seethed, watching the riots on Fox News with her arms crossed and her shoulders up.

He nervously sat down next to her on the sofa one night and asked, "Do you need to talk about this?"

Her shoulders were up again and her jaw clenched.

"There's not much to be said," she sighed glumly.

"I guess we can both agree things are crazy right now. It's out of any of our hands," Stephe admitted.

"I just don't understand how people can be so wrong," she said sadly.

"The problem is we can't agree on who's wrong and who's right," Stephe said.

"I guess we'll just have to agree to disagree."

"Can you do that?" he asked.

"I'll have to."

"Well, just know that Jack and I love you. And some day all of this will calm down again."

"I hope."

One night after work in February, 2032, Stephe had to publish a story on another gay nightclub shooting in New Orleans in which fourteen people were killed. He was to meet up with Nona for dinner at Catch in the Castro. He'd been looking forward to it all week; there wasn't any money for eating in restaurants anymore, but they'd decided to splurge. Nona was late. She finally surprised him at their designated meeting spot in Powell Street BART and Muni Station.

It was rush hour, the place was packed. All the white tile of the station still gleamed; things felt normal.

They Muoned through the fare gates and were on the escalator down to the Muni platform when a suicide bomber blew himself up, upstairs in the middle of the station, where the crowd was the heaviest.

To Stephe and Nona it was as if someone had turned the air into a weapon. A fierce wall of pressure threw them backwards onto the escalator, knocking them over. Full of shrapnel and bits of body, the very air seemed to turn red. The escalator kept going; soon there was a tangle of dazed and bleeding people piling up at the bottom with more being dumped in every second. Stephe managed to right himself and pulled Nona up, too, but not before stepping on someone's hand.

As they pulled people up from the escalator an inbound L-Taraval car beeped, closed its doors and drove out of the station, unaware of the carnage upstairs.

Shrapnel and bodies were everywhere. Stephe and Nona hugged each other and found that they were a little banged up—nicks and burns on both of their faces and on Nona's arms, all bleeding. Stephe took off his overshirt and daubed at Nona's face.

For a while there was nowhere to go. After a BART train was heard departing downstairs, the station was quickly closed. There was no going back upstairs—where the blast had occurred—so they did what they could, checking to see that the people around them were okay. People were blindly milling about in the confusion, unsure of what to do. Stephe encouraged everyone to sit down where they were and to wait for help to arrive. It seemed like an eternity passed before they heard sirens—then more sirens, a constant wail from upstairs. Police and EMT personnel finally made their way down the still-moving escalator to suss out damage and injuries. Everyone down below had mostly superficial injuries; Stephe and Nona were finally escorted back upstairs.

Leaving, they had to walk through the bomb blast zone. It was unholy carnage. Gone was the gleaming white tile; blood was everywhere. Nona buried her face in Stephe's chest and they walked that way, sideways, hugging each other, until they were clear of the station and out into an aid car. They were triaged to Zuckerberg Hospital with burns and shrapnel to the face and arms.

Sixty-eight people died in the blast. Hundreds were injured. Neo-Nazis took credit for the blast, as did a faction of the Freedom Fighters.

Simultaneously, a suicide bomber blew herself up in Los Angeles' Union Station. One hundred and one people were killed there.

It had a polarizing effect. Calls for California's secession grew louder.

As the depression raged on, Stephe was fairly insulated. He kept his job, although half the staff was let go. The entire archival department was dissolved so Stephe had to serve in that capacity as well—simply filing his reports and dumping them into boxes to be sorted later. Margery managed to keep her job, although a good number of nurses were laid off, throwing an insane and unsafe work load onto the remaining staff. Margery was getting older and ready for retirement, yet she wasn't sure she had a retirement left to look forward to.

Jack lost his job at the law firm and came back to live at 472 Liberty Street in his old room; he and Elena stayed together in their relationship, but he refused to live with her if he couldn't pay his part.

The nation braced itself for the 2032 presidential election. Kellum ran against a Democratic nominee named Brittany Marsh. People joked endlessly at the prospect of a president named "Brittany."

But they joked even more bitterly that the votes would be rigged again and that President Brittany didn't have a chance.

On the 2032 ballot was an initiative to split California from the Union. Kellum said he'd send the Army if he had to—which actually had the opposite effect. California wanted out. The people of California were liberal and rich; they had agriculture and technology. They had the entertainment and aeronautics industries. The California economy was always ten paces ahead of the rest of the country and had held on to liberal governments unimpeded since Arnold Schwarzenegger left office in 2011. The people of California wanted environmental legislation, healthcare, and education—all the things the rest of the U.S. had abandoned.

The state certainly had its conservative elements; much of California was agricultural and people outside the big cities watched Fox News and voted red. But they were far fewer in number than the liberals. Many conservatives chose not to stay, moving out of California just as so many liberals flooded in.

Mitch Kellum won the popular vote in 2032 and California became an independent country.

Everything had to be set up from scratch. California needed its own customs and immigration/border patrol. They needed a stock market, a currency. An army and a navy.

The Pacific Stock Exchange in San Francisco, closed in 2001, roared back to life. The California Dollar, at first pegged to the U.S. dollar, was then set afloat where it quickly gained in value, while the U.S. dollar continued to sink.

Sixty-eight year old Kamala Harris was voted first President of California.

In the failing U.S., people flocked to big cities at an unprecedented rate. Generally liberal, cities felt like safe havens. The biggest obstacle was money: The cities were far more expensive, out of the reach of many.

Emboldened by California's success, New York, Boston, Philadelphia, and Baltimore set up the concept of Bubble Cities; liberal enclaves that responded less and less to federal demands for cooperation. Or for tax revenue. Finally, in 2033, in a stinging rebuke, the Eastern Seaboard Cities told the United States to go to hell. They set themselves up as Bubble Cities, officially called an Autonomous City Regions, or ACRs. Other cities soon followed suit: Chicago, Denver, Portland, Seattle, Minneapolis-St. Paul, Austin, Columbus. Once again Kellum threatened to send troops, but it became increasingly unclear as to who his troops were. The U.S. military was as fractured as the government; each military base quietly pledged fealty to their own region over the country at large.

One by one each ACR declared itself independent of the United States. Kellum was powerless to stop it. He didn't have an army anymore. A general currency was established and shared between the Eastern Seaboard and the Bubble Cities, set apart from the sagging U.S. dollar.

Washington, DC, would have been part of the Eastern Seaboard ACR, but as the seat of the U.S. government, it wound up being a hybrid city: Liberal in many respects, but the powerhouse of the government. A line was drawn in the sand; Kellum vowed any attempt to take Washington, DC, would be met with force. And nobody wanted to mess up the furniture. So DC remained part of the U.S.

Mass migration followed the establishments of California and the ACRs; many Conservative people chose to leave. But far greater numbers were flocking to the Bubble Cities in hopes of jobs and a better life. Quickly the borders closed. The Bubble Cities became walled citadels: they couldn't handle the hordes of people seeking asylum. Border camps grew up outside the cities, full of refugees waiting for their chance that their Muons would clear and they'd be given the green light to enter the cities.

California also had to enact strict border controls. All highways had Customs Stations set up within the first few weeks, but with 2,050 miles of open border, people could just walk in. And they did. Border crossings of refugees became a huge problem. Most were caught by Muon and deported. Some people cut their Muons out, but that didn't work for long—you couldn't do anything socially or economically without one.

It was a great polarization. Liberal Bubble Cities thrived. Social Security and Medicare for all were quickly put into place. Universities were free. They did what they could to re-enact environmental legislations. Gay marriage was reinstated, civil rights reasserted.

For everyone else out in rural America, they got what they wanted, too: In particular, a Christian state. Rid of the pesky liberals, they were free to be conservative and proud. The New U.S. was happier; they could go about their business of polluting and pillaging. Corporations controlled everything. Kellum held onto power over his remaining, limping country.

The Culture War was over.

Chapter 14

Despite the backdrop of horror, even though U.S. society was on the brink of collapse, science advanced at an exponential rate. Several cures for cancer were found—although no one in the U.S. could afford them—and stem cell research surged forward, cloning technology, artificial intelligence, and driverless cars. And Muons.

Cold Fusion Reactors and solar power—coupled with batteries of a hundredfold capacity—solved the energy problems in Russia, India, China, Europe and Canada. But the U.S. was slow to adapt, steadfastly sticking to coal and nuclear fission, and senselessly drilling the arctic for oil. Too much money was at stake. Oil was becoming obsolete to everyone except the Americans, and it kept the U.S. in thrall to the Middle East, whose politics hadn't improved in the slightest.

China, India and Russia banded together and revolutionized space propulsion. Ion thrust and fusion drives were devised. Travel time to the Moon was down to 456 minutes— a little more than seven and a half hours. Mars was nine days away. Io, Titan and Europa were just a month away. As life on Earth hardened and flopped, space became a boomtown. The Moon and Mars were colonized.

The hardest part had always been getting into orbit. Traditional chemical rockets were expensive and still had a tendency to blow up. They could burn for only about nine minutes, long enough to reach orbit, but then their fuel was spent, leaving them lifeless.

Several new ways were found. The most profitable were space planes: Huge aircraft would super-sonic their way into the stratosphere and launch an ion driven vehicle into orbit for a fraction of the cost. Getting into orbit was still the most expensive part of space flight, but the costs came down and demand went up.

Several space stations came into being; the ISS quadrupled in size.

Apple™ Station opened for business in 2033. The ultimate business center, it provided offices with one hell of a view. It became Apple Headquarters.

The Moon became important. It contained vast amounts of Helium-3—rare on Earth, indispensable for cold fusion reactors. The moon was also rich in Rare Earth Minerals (REMs) which became increasingly needed in the manufacture of modern electronics.

The need for Helium-3 became so great, and the cost of travel to the Moon so low, that economics quickly kicked in and interplanetary travel soon became the norm.

Like the old gold rushes of California and Alaska, at first only the most greedy and intrepid corporations flew to the Moon to mine Helium-3. But with them went suppliers and hookers and tourists, and people liked it there because it didn't have all the problems of Old Earth. It became a status symbol. It was made cheaper by technology. They burned Helium-3 to go to the Moon to get more Helium-3 to go to the Moon . . . to get more Helium-3.

The Moon was literally made of building materials: concrete. So palaces grew. Titans of industry made their homes on the Moon. It became the Hamptons, without the burdens of full gravity. It was the ultimate status symbol.

Chapter 15

By 2034 the economies of California and the Bubble Cities stabilized. Stephe held on to his job at the Gay Liberation Front. The Archive department roared back to life with several of its old staff members brought back, and with two new years of horror stories to document and file. Hundreds of gay men and women had died in the Culture War, and for those remaining in the old U.S., the situation continued to be bleak. It was still Stephe's job to report on what was happening in the United States. He saw it first-hand.

On a Saturday night in August, 2034, two gunmen shot up the Woodshed Lounge at 4000 Queen City Drive in Charlotte, North Carolina. Just like the Orlando Pulse massacre of 2017, the Throckmorton Mining Company Dallas in 2029 and Oscar's in Palm Springs the year before, two neo-Nazi/Freedom Fighters shot the place up, killing thirty-four people. The very next day the LGBT Community Center on Hamilton Street was firebombed in the night.

Stephe's boss, David, called him into his office.

"We're sending you to Charlotte," David said.

"Wait. You want *me* to go to South Carolina?" Stephe gulped.

David smiled. "Actually, it's *North* Carolina, and yes, we do.

"My God, what for?" Stephe was aghast.

"Since the firebombing and massacre this weekend they need someone from the National Level there giving support and gathering information. We want someone on the ground to write up what's going on. You're our best reporter. We want you to meet with Patricia McIntyre—she's the head of the LGBT Community Center. It's just for a day and a half. We think it'll be good. For them and for us. Take them some screens, get 'em started back up again."

Stephe gulped again.

"And there's no way out of it?" Stephe asked hopefully.

"Nope. You're on the 7 a.m. plane tomorrow. Go ahead and take the rest of today off; I want you to be at your best."

"Thanks. I guess."

Stephe worked to wrap his head around it. He was petrified.

He left the office and headed slowly for home. He picked up some Chinese food on his way. He called Nona.

"I have to go to Charlotte, North Carolina, tomorrow. To interview the people. And bring screens."

"Are you scared?" she asked.

"Yes!" he exclaimed. "They're still killing people out there!"

"I know. This is huge."

"It's incredibly huge. I don't want to go; I wonder if David is trying to get rid of me, to put me in harm's way," Stephe suggested.

"He wouldn't really do that," Nona said reassuringly. "I know he doesn't like you, but he wouldn't knowingly put you in danger."

"I suppose. But I'm scared as hell. I've never been to the South, and I can't imagine being in the U.S. again. It's unnerving."

"You wanna get some dinner? I'm buying," Nona offered.

"Naw, thanks, I got some Mongu-ro ngao fung at Sam's, I'm just gonna eat that."

"Okay. When do you come back?" she asked.

Stephe replied, "David says it's just a day and a half, so.... Thursday?"

"Do you want to take a gun?" Nona asked.

"Where would I find one around here? Besides I'd probably just shoot my own balls off."

"You don't want that," Nona laughed.

"No. Anyway I'll text you when I'm there, okay?" Stephe replied.

"Yes, please do. Stay in touch, call if you need to, no matter what time it is. And good luck! I'm sure you'll be fine,"

"Thanks!"

They said goodbye and hung up.

The next morning he took a driverless Uber to SFO and flew from San Francisco to Washington Dulles; flight time 2 and a half hours, because planes were faster. There was no rail service to Charlotte anymore; the High Speed Systems had collapsed after the Culture War, so he flew in a very old jet, an Embraer 205, to Charlotte.

Customs didn't want to let him into the U.S. They took him to a room and asked him his income ($1,250,000 U.S.), race and party affiliation. All of which was available on his Muon; they were just being dicks about it. "Liberal . . . we don't much go for that around here," the U.S. officer grunted. They asked three times how long he was staying. Any plans to stay longer?

"No," was all Stephe could stammer. It was giving him the creeps. Finally they let him go and he stepped out onto U.S. soil for the first time since the Secession.

Charlotte was well beyond the Bubble Cities. He was in the Deep South. They were still driving vehicles that burned gas. He went to the curb; a limo was supposed to take him to his hotel. Finally he saw his name on a screen; a diffident elderly

African-American man tipped his hat and called him "Sir" and walked him to the limo—a pretty nice Lincoln Town Car. But the vehicle was at least twenty years old, the engine was running roughly and smoke was coming from the tailpipe. Stephe settled into the back seat as the driver, who introduced himself as Fergus, took the wheel and drove it manually.

It was a short ride to the Sheraton; cars, all gas-powered and most on manual drive, jammed the streets, and it seemed surprisingly normal. When they got to the Sheraton, Fergus opened his door, popped the trunk and pulled out Stephe's suitcase. Stephe Muoned him $300 U.S., and Fergus shook his hand and welcomed him to Charlotte.

The desk clerk welcomed him as well. The place hadn't been redecorated in a long time, and still reeked of turn-of-the century charm. He checked in and was given room 329. The number was beamed to his Muon. He waved his wrist over the door sensor and it snicked open.

His meeting wasn't until next morning so he took a shower—another $300 U.S for the water—and lounged on the bed. He texted Nona and realized he was very lonely and nervous. He was in a dangerous place all by himself: in a strange hotel, in a strange city, in what was now a very strange country. He didn't want to be there.

He pulled up Growlr, a dating app on his Muon, just for someone to talk to. A local who could put his mind at ease and, he supposed, could be an interview while he was at it. At any rate, he'd feel less lonely.

There were a few brave souls still online despite the political climate. He tried to strike up a few chat conversations, but was ignored by several; a couple of guys just wanted sex and flashed him naked pictures, but he just wasn't in the mood.

One cute bearish guy named Fallow Ranch was more in the mood to chat. His real name was Jeremy. He worked on a pig farm and was clearly rattled by the massacre.

"I'm really really freaked out," he wrote. "It's just so scary and senseless. I'm glad I don't go out to bars much, but I've been in the Woodshed. I was there just last week. It could of been me."

"I live in San Francisco. Was at Powell Street Station for the bombing. So I know what you mean," Stephe wrote on his screen to Jeremy.

"No shit? Wow. What's it like living in San Francisco?"

"It's good. Expensive as hell."

Stephe went downstairs for cocktails and dinner, still conversing with Jeremy on his Muon. He asked a lot of questions about what life was like in North Carolina, during the Culture War and after.

Jeremy was really good to talk to. Stephe was feeling much less alone and anxious. A few guys still beeped in looking for sex, and Stephe politely told them he wasn't into hooking up; they quickly went away.

After a few scotches, though, he was really warming up to Jeremy. And vice-versa, he could tell. Jeremy, like Stephe, didn't do a lot of hooking up and was looking for a man to love.

"It's almost impossible to meet guys here," Jeremy wrote. "Mostly real hot straight bubbas and a whole lot of neo-Nazis. I don't really have anywhere to turn. Now that the Woodshed is gone, I don't s'pose I ever will."

"Did you know anyone at the Woodshed?"

"A few. Not real well. There was this one guy I really had the hots for. He was never interested. And now he's dead."

"I find it so hard to wrap my head around."

"I know."

"And frankly I can't believe someone wasn't interested in you," Stephe wrote. "You're adorable, if you don't mind me saying."

Blush emoji. "Thanks! I like talking to you."

"Likewise!"

"Where you staying at?"

"The Sheraton by the airport. It's pretty lonely here."

"Fancy!"

"It's not bad."

"Do you want me to come over?" Jeremy asked. "We could have a drink."

Stephe was floored, but excited at the prospect.

"You'd do that? I think that would be cool. It would be great to meet you."

"I think so. You seem like a nice guy."

After two scotches Stephe was ready for anything. It wasn't what he'd planned on, but Jeremy was such a sweet guy, and Stephe found him absolutely adorable. They unlocked their pics for each other, and both agreed that Jeremy would come over.

Stephe brushed his teeth and lay on the bed in his bathrobe; he tried to watch TV to distract himself but nothing was on but junk and local news, which was pretty sickening right-wing propaganda.

After thirty minutes there was a light tapping on the door to room 329.

Stephe looked through the peephole. Jeremy was all bear; short, stocky, with a blonde beard. A definite catch! Stephe wondered nervously if he was to Jeremy's liking as he opened the door and Jeremy came in. As if to answer, Jeremy leaned up and began kissing Stephe, his short warm tongue darting hungrily in Stephe's mouth. The door closed and they embraced, their heavy breathing and beards scratching the only sounds in the room. Finally they parted, Jeremy's hand went to Stephe's open robe and grabbed on, much pulsing and warm grip. They went to the bed and explored each other all over.

So much for drinks and conversation, Stephe mused.

He delighted in holding Jeremy. He was squat and covered in golden fur and was amazing to touch, to hold, to smell.

They made love. It was heavenly.

"Dayamm!" Jeremy grunted as they finished; Jeremy rolled onto his back. "That was nice!" He said it like "nahce." Even his accent was cute. Stephe plopped down beside him, his head in the crook of Jeremy's armpit. They were sweaty and warm.

"So yer from San Francisco?" Jeremy asked.

"Yup. Born and raised, same house since birth," Stephe answered.

"You were there for the earthquake?"

"Sure was. My parents were killed in Millennium Tower. It was pretty rough."

"Shit! I'm so sorry." Jeremy leaned over and gave Stephe a kiss on the forehead. "I wish I could go to California," he said. "My sister tried to get in but was refused. She's in Arizona now, still trying."

"I hear it's pretty rough out there."

"She's not in a camp. She got a job in Phoenix, trying to save up enough money to try again. Like everyone else in Phoenix; that's why they call it God's Waiting Room." Jeremy used a bit of bed sheet to wipe off his midsection. "It's been pretty quiet here, we haven't had any problems in a long time. Until this week."

"That's good," Stephe said. "Have you been through a lot before?"

"I was caught in a food riot in Charlotte last year; it was pretty scary. People stormed the food court at a mall I was at. By the time the riot police got there it was over and done with, but a few shots were fired."

"Dang!"

"Y'all don't have that problem in California, do ya?"

"No, other than the bombing, things are pretty good. Our Culture War riots were over quickly. The Freedom Fighters knew they were outnumbered and didn't put up much of a fight."

"I stayed away from the Culture War. A lot of people in Charlotte died that week, but I stayed on the farm and kept out of it."

"Smart."

"Still I know a lot of people who got into fights, on both sides. No one's speaking to anyone anymore. So you're here to cover the massacre?" Jeremy asked.

"Yeah, I'm a writer."

"Cool."

"Yeah. It's cool." Stephe craned his head up and began kissing Jeremy again. "You're welcome to spend the night."

"I'd like that," Jeremy replied with his gentle Southern lilt. "Gotta get up super early though."

They bedded down for the night. It felt good to be next to a warm body under the cool air conditioner, and Stephe slept well.

Chapter 16

Jeremy was gone when Stephe woke up with a start to his alarm. He felt a loneliness at the empty space beside him in the bed. But Jeremy had beamed a note with his phone number and email to Stephe's Muon. "In case you come back!" with a smiley face.

With a sigh Stephe put some coffee on and took another $300 shower.

His day started with a meeting with the staff of The Gay Center that had been firebombed two days before. The meeting was, as he expected, a sober affair. He met Patricia McIntyre, his host for the day. She was a brunette in her fifties.

"We're lucky," Patricia explained. "They bombed us at night. We're a staff of six with clients in and out all day, so, if they'd wanted to kill people, they sure missed their chance. I don't think we could handle any more death around here."

She continued: "Of course, we get no end of death threats; emails, phone calls, and hate mail. We have an armed security guard there during the day, but at night it's just an empty house."

"What did the police say?" Stephe asked.

Patricia laughed bitterly. "They basically said, 'Better luck next time.' They promised to send it up to the FBI, but I don't think that'll happen."

They drove over to the bombed out house; Stephe looked around, did a short video report, holding his own screen up. There wasn't much left to the place.

Then they toured the Woodshed Lounge. It was alarming. Thirty-four people had been gunned down inside three days before and Stephe didn't want to go in. Dried blood still stained the floor.

He interviewed survivors of the Woodshed Lounge on video for the GLF.

Scott was in the DJ booth:

I saw them come in. They didn't look right in black trench coats on a hot night. They went up to the bar, had a couple of drinks and then just started shooting. You could barely hear the shots over the music. I froze. I guess it was stupid of me, I should have dove for cover but they ignored me and just started gunning everyone down. It took a while for people to realize what was going on, I guess, but then there was a stampede for the doors. I don't know anything about guns but whatever they were shooting was powerful. It just blasted people in two, and mowed through the folks piled up at the doors trying to get out. That's when I cut the music and dove for cover. So I didn't see anything after that. Just heard the rattle of machine gun shots. I don't know how it ended, except I heard they got away.

After ten minutes of complete silence I climbed down from the DJ booth and saw all the bodies. I didn't think anybody was alive in there, they were cut up too bad. So I ran out the back door, half expecting to get blown away, but whoever they were, they were gone. I was in the full parking lot behind the bar and looking at all those cars, that's when it hit me. The cars didn't belong to anybody anymore. They're all still there in the parking lot.

Next Stephe interviewed an African-American guy named Derreck:

I'm a bartender; it was a busy night, a good crowd. Mostly regulars. Two men in black came in and they actually came up to the bar and ordered double bourbons. They weren't regular, I didn't think they belonged in there; they looked like they were straight, dressed in black with light trench coats on, which was unusual since it was so damned hot out. But that's where they hid their machine guns. As soon as they downed their bourbons, they nodded to each other and reached into their trench coats. I was more concerned that they weren't volunteering to pay for their drinks for a second, then I realized what they were doing. I yelled "Look out!" and dove under the bar, but of course no one could hear me over the music.

They opened fire. I could barely hear the shots ringing out because of the music and I couldn't see anything. They fired at where I'd just been standing a second before—the shots shattered and blasted everything all to hell. There's a refrigerator under the bar, I was behind that. I guess they started walking around shooting everybody. They fired back at me but the bullets didn't penetrate the fridge. It saved my life. I heard screams and bloodshed and could hear that they were making their way to the door.

I can't believe they got away, but they did. People are saying they just jumped into an old pick-up truck and drove off.

The police were here in about five minutes and then the news showed up too. The whole thing only lasted about two minutes and then they were gone.

I had to stay for hours, being interviewed by the police and the media. Finally at about 1:30 I was allowed to go home. I didn't lock the place up. There wasn't any need. Doors were open and paramedics carrying out the bodies.

You could hear everybody's phones ringing, all around the floor where the bodies lay.

"I lost a lot of friends, hiding behind that fridge," Derreck said, breaking into tears. "It's just so horrible and senseless."

Stephe gave him a hug and held him while he sobbed.

He wished he weren't there; anywhere but there.

He interviewed the police. A spokeswoman in a business suit. She sounded bored and not interested. Yes, they're looking for the suspects. No, they don't have any leads except the stolen Ford 250 pick-up they drove away in was found a day later in a Safeway parking lot in Gastonia. They'd obviously used the two-car method. She said something catty about, if gay guys want to flaunt it in public, they'd better be prepared to pay the price. Pursed lips.

"Are you saying we should just stay home and out of sight?" Stephe asked her.

"No, but don't go prancing around. People get the wrong idea."

Stephe and Patricia got interviewed on CNN and MSNBC. Fox News was not present.

There was one final meeting with the Gay Center group as a whole and they were done by 4:30 that afternoon. Stephe had just enough time to grab his overnight bag and head back to the airport.

He witnessed some sort of police incident alongside the road, where he saw three African-American men lined up and shot. The police just blew them away. Stephe was helpless in the backseat of his limo; the driver didn't stop and Stephe didn't think the driver even saw what had happened.

He never knew what it was about; he checked the local newsfeeds and no mention was ever made.

Stephe was able to make his flight to Dulles and then the transcon back home. He got out of Customs and Immigration at SFO by 8 p.m., Ubered home, and was back in his childhood house by 9 p.m. He sent an email to Jeremy, with all honesty hoping he'd see him again. But the thought of all those people being shot haunted him as he tried to sleep in his parent's bedroom at the top of the stairs.

Chapter 17

Charlotte was just the first of many.

Stephe became the go-to reporter for horror at the Gay Liberation Front. Time and time again, he'd have to fly to the U.S. for a massacre, an outrage, or a lynching. Times too numerous to count.

He was almost always flagged in customs.

The hardest for him was the lynching of six gay men in Jacksonville, Florida. The bodies were still strung up in the trees when he got there, as if the police couldn't be bothered to cut them down or they wanted to make sure someone from the GLF would get a clear picture of it.

Stephe became just one of the reporters; MSNBC, CNN, Fox—they'd all get called out as witnesses. America loved its news, and each occurrence made headlines. But Stephe was there in a special capacity—not just as a reporter, but as an archivist and activist. He was there for support. Just having the GLF on hand seemed to make a difference for the bereaved. The numbers of the many bereaved were growing quickly. It had become a nightmare.

Gay rights continued to erode. And Stephe, perhaps more than any one person in California, had to see it up close.

A typical Tuesday at the office in 2035, Stephe was working on a particularly heartrending gay hate crime in Bloomington, Indiana. He got invited by Nicole and Craig and a girl named Kaitlin to go to the Elite Café on Upper Fillmore for drinks. Stephe was just going to work late, as he did nearly every night, but he needed to get out and meet more people. So the four of them took the California street car to Fillmore, went in and got a table.

Stephe noticed the man right away: a gray bearded, handsome fellow at the bar with two women, and eventually they came over and sat at the next table. Stephe's Muon *Click!*ed. Which he didn't even need—he could just tell.

His group of four—and Hot Guy's group of three—gradually melded into a group of seven, talking politics. They were discussing the skirmishes at the California border as tons of people still tried to immigrate in. The shambles that was the remaining United States under President Kellum. Reciprocal agreements with the U.S. for food and technology and how it was a very uneasy truce. How most of the U.S. was rural, agricultural, and racist as hell. No healthcare, bad infrastructure, constantly teetering between recession and full-on depression. They talked about how the ACRs and California sent a lot in aid in exchange for agriculture, although California itself was nearly self-sustaining.

One of the women with Hot Guy had made it through the border in Arizona the hard way. She spoofed her ID in Phoenix—it cost her a fortune, with no guarantees that it would actually work. Well, it got her across the border in Blythe but it timed out in three months.

"Took a lot of lawyers and dough to get it straightened out," she laughed. She was pretty. Brown wavy hair and a sexy blue dress. "Anything was better than staying in Omaha." Her levity faded when she mentioned that her parents were killed in the Culture War. "Still," she sighed, "I'm glad to be among the land of the living and free of the Flyover States of America!" And she raised her glass and was toasted by all.

Stephe kept making eye contact with Mr. Tall Grey and Rugged, and he finally broke the ice: "So what's your story?" relieved that he was finally going to get the chance to talk to him.

"I'm Max Brewer," he said in a marvelous, resonant voice. He looked Stephe right in the eye; he had a very direct, unflinching gaze and icy blue eyes. "I'm lucky, I grew up in Pasadena. So no stories to tell, really, just an interior designer born and raised on the Interior. Cheers!" They all raised their glasses again.

"I was born and raised here—same house from birth," Stephe volunteered. "Lost my parents at Millennium Tower and I've been here ever since."

Several people made sighs and Max put his hand on Stephe's knee. "I'm so sorry," he said in that magnificent voice of his. But the feeling of his hand on Stephe's knee sent a thrill through him. Max was looking at him intently with a shy, sad smile. Their Muons mutually *Click!*ed.

Stephe told his tales of going to the Hinterland so often, and of his work at the GLF. As usual he played it down; it was a buzzkill to overshare. He made jokes about what it was like, constantly having to go through Customs into the U.S. and all the dumb things the bubba border guards always asked.

They took turns telling their tales. Nicole was the life of the table with raucous descriptions of her sex change. Craig got out his screen and showed everyone pictures of his son.

He had grown up in Vallejo and was part of the demonstration that ran the Freedom Fighters out of San Francisco. Kaitlin had been in California since 2028, raised in Seattle. The other girl with Max, Tish, was from Chicago, so immigrating was easy. It's much less a hassle to come to California from a Bubble City. She arrived just this year and worked in marketing.

All in all it was nice; one of those spontaneous evenings that works out like a house afire. They decided to order food, pushing the two round tables together as best they could, and conversation flowed. Stephe had shrimp in cream pasta.

He kept looking at Max; Max kept looking at him.

"Interior design, huh? I'd hate for you to see my place: It's decorated in what I call "Early Craigslist." Everyone laughed.

"Well, I got started early," Max said, his keen and intent gaze on Stephe. "I kept rearranging my parents' furniture and rehanging their art, so my mom suggested I become an interior designer. After ten years of meaningless jobs, I finally went to school at UCLA and moved up here in 2022."

"So you were here for the quake?" Stephe asked.

"Sure the hell was!" Max responded. "I'd just moved here for a job two weeks before. I was at my office in downtown Oakland; Christ, it was a mess! All the glass shattered, and the shaking was so violent that everything—and I mean *everything*—was thrown off my desk and onto the floor. The building had to be torn down, you could actually see individual bricks in the walls dancing. One wall caved in completely. It was an old place, built in the 1920s. I'll always miss that building; it had a lot of charm."

"So how old are you, if you don't mind me asking?" Stephe inquired.

"Forty-two next month. I'm a Cancer," Max proclaimed.

"I'm an Aquarius; I'm only twenty-seven."

"Ah. Chicken! I wish I were twenty-seven again, knowing what I know now." He winked.

Max was beautiful to Stephe. Close-cropped greying hair, shocking blue eyes, and a long gray beard halfway down his chest. Stephe couldn't help but check out the nipples. Pierced. He could see them through Max's t-shirt. Broad shoulders, muscular arms. Beefy thighs from what he could make out.

The dinner was drawing to a close; The group broke up on the sidewalk, Max taking the women with him north on Fillmore to his car, Stephe's group each heading back to their respective homes.

"I wouldn't mind seeing you again," Stephe said nervously to Max.

"I'd like that," he said.

They Muoned each other their email addresses and hugged it out on the sidewalk. Stephe appreciated the hug, it was nice.

He took the 22 Fillmore bus down to the Castro, Muoning his fare of twenty-eight dollars. Got home to find Margery in the kitchen.

"How was your evening," she asked.

"It was grand! Thanks. I met some very interesting people. How was work?"

"Oh, same. My favorite patient, the one I told you about, got to be released today; I was very glad for her."

"That's good! A happy story."

"Indeed."

That night he texted Max: "Would you like to get coffee some night this week?"

"Sure! I'm free Friday night," came Max's response.

"I'll keep it open. I'll ink you in—no pencil!" Stephe replied.

Stephe was ecstatic. He really liked Max, although he didn't know a thing about him. He was hot, what could he say? Just the right balance of sensitive and rugged.

Friday rolled around and, texting back and forth, they'd decided to forego coffee and have dinner. A good sign. Max lived in Dogpatch, a fairly remote corner of the city, so he came to the Castro. They met at Starbucks and walked to Sausage Factory for spaghetti.

"I'm actually a PoliSci major, but with a minor in interior design," Max explained. "Interior design is my passion, PoliSci is my job. I work for the Federal Government of California, constantly on the High-Speed back and forth to Sacramento. I work for the Secretary of State in the Registrar of Voters."

"I've heard all the hype, but never understood. So millions of people in the U.S. who voted by Muon simply had their votes hacked in 2030?" Stephe asked.

"Basically. It was a rout. Muons are much more easily spoofed than people want to believe. Half a dozen groups were responsible for the fraud: Republicans, mostly; the Russians, the Chinese, half a dozen kids in their parents' basement. That's why we are launching campaigns to revert to old style paper ballots. Each state has to do this according to their own rules and guidelines. I'm in charge of California—well, I'm not in *charge*, but that's the bulk of my job," Max said, then he asked, "What about you? How do you stay sane in your job? I couldn't handle it."

"Sometimes I can't," Stephe admitted.

"Jesus. I mean, I read about it but it's so hard to put into perspective; to believe it's real, you know what I mean?"

"Yeah. I know," Stephe agreed.

They ordered their spaghetti and a bottle of red wine.

Conversation turned to other things. "I'm just out of a four-year relationship," Max said. "Ended about eight months ago. I got dumped."

"Jesus, I'm sorry," Stephe said, and on a whim, reached his hand across the table and held Max's hand. He didn't pull away.

"Thanks. It was pretty rough. His name was Mike and he ditched me for a younger, Brazilian model. Their Muons *Click!*ed and off he went."

"I find that so hard to believe. You're like really hot."

Max blushed a little. "Thanks," he said again.

"So tell me about Pasadena."

"Well, what can be said about it? It's a pretty boring part of L.A. Nice old houses. It was pretty quiet growing up there. I always knew I wanted to be in the Bay Area, so as soon as I finished at UCLA I headed up. Just in time for the earthquake."

"What did you do during the aftermath?"

"I was new in town, so I didn't have any friends to crash with. I wound up in a tent city at Lake Merritt for a few days but couldn't hack it, so I went back down to L.A. and stayed with my parents for a year. There was no point in looking for housing that first year, not in the Bay Area, so I basically waited it out. But I knew I wanted to be back here. As soon as I could get an apartment, I did. The Bay Area lost a lot of its character and charm that day. But a city is what the people make it; I aim to stay here."

"I'm glad," Stephe ventured.

"What about you? Where were you when it happened?"

Stephe told the tale of being in gym class in high school.

"High school? Jesus, how young are you???" Max laughed.

"Not just high school, but a *freshman* in high school. I'm still chicken, remember?"

"And you lost your parents."

"Yeah," Stephe said glumly. "It was fucking hard. I walked home alone to an empty house. Kept waiting for word; no electricity, no phones. It was torture. They were officially declared dead about two weeks later. It was pretty bleak. My brother Jack flew home from Chicago and our Aunt Margery came in from Colorado to take care of us. It was a very dark time," Stephe said. "We're all still in the house. It was my parent's house, paid for, survived the fires, so it's been a sort of nexus for me my whole life. I'll probably always stay there."

"I'd like to see it," Max said.

Stephe blushed. "I'd be glad to show it to you. It's only a couple of blocks away."

"That must be nice, living in the heart of the Castro— even though the Castro isn't the Castro anymore."

They finished up by sharing a crême brulée and having one more glass of red wine. Then they set out in the night air and walked up the steep hill to 472 Liberty Street.

They sat in the living room on the old couch that had been there for twenty years. Not much of the house was changed; no one had been in the mood. Margery certainly didn't have a flair for decorating, Jack wasn't interested and Stephe liked things the way they were.

Stephe asked Max what he'd do to the living room if he were given a free hand—"Unless I'm asking for free advice; you're a professional. I'm not looking for a freebie."

"Well, I'd play up the Victorian aspect. Although, technically, the house is Edwardian. Bring out the woodwork and a few sconces."

"I like that you can say the word 'sconce' in a sentence and still be butch."

"Grrrr," Max growled.

"I took my parents' room at the top floor. Decorated it last year. I'd been living in the same room my whole life; it was kind of time to get rid of the Star Wars posters and Sponge Bob flannel sheets."

Max blanched. "God," he said.

"Would you like to see it?" Stephe asked.

It was only 8:30 on this Friday night, but Max said, "Sure!" and they climbed the steps to the top of the house.

"Not bad," Max declared, examining the room. "You made some good choices. There's hope for you yet!"

They embraced, standing in the middle of the room and Max, being somewhat taller, leaned down and gave Stephe a kiss. A good kiss. French. No piercings. Max was so barrel-chested that Stephe had to put one foot back just to stay in position. They leaned in, forehead to forehead, holding each other. He smelled his breath. Garlic and red wine. Max was a hunk. A good fifty pounds heavier than Stephe; very solid. He had such a beautiful long flowing gray beard. They made out in the middle of the room for several minutes, just kissing and holding and exploring with hands. Stephe knew that since Max's nipples were large and pierced that they would be a button for him and, in this, he was not wrong. He pulled up Max's t-shirt and chewed on his nipples, eliciting a low moan for Max.

Finally they broke and headed for the four-poster bed at the peak of the house.

Stephe disrobed. They climbed into the bed which creaked under their weight and explored each other's bodies. Stephe couldn't imagine this man getting dumped eight months ago. Insane! They kissed and tweaked each other's nipples; they just surfed each other's bodies.

They made passionate love, trying each other on for size. Max was heavenly. A definite keeper. Stephe saw stars, he came so hard.

"Woooooff!" growled Max, rolling over onto his back.

Stephe was used to shutting down immediately after climaxing but he didn't feel that way with Max. They sighed and relaxed.

"God *damn*, that was fine!" Max said.

"Damn straight!" said Stephe.

"Grrr," Max playfully growled.

They kissed deeply, sloppily, warmly.

Stephe pulled back the covers on the bed and climbed in. Max followed. Soon they were embracing under the covers, talking in low, husky, post-coital whispers.

"I can't believe someone dumped you. What are you, an asshole or something?"

"Sometimes I can be," Max admitted bravely. "What about you; any great loves?"

"A few crushes. Nothing long-term. I've been a bachelor for years now. There were a few in college I would have kept, but they had other plans."

"Men are bitches," Max said.

"Aye, lad. That they are," responded Stephe. Max's head was in the crook of his arm so Stephe kissed him atop his head, smelling the close-cropped gray hair, still a little sweaty from their lovemaking.

Lovemaking. Stephe smiled. That's what it was, all right. And it was good.

Max stayed the night; Stephe awoke next morning to Max pawing at him ready for another go. They went at it hot and heavy, better than the night before. Max was a tiger in bed.

Stephe threw on a robe, got them some coffee from the kitchen, and they lay in bed talking. Favorite things, what things you hate, how do you like to be treated; how can you not tolerate being treated? They had a lot in common.

"I just can't handle criticism or being yelled at in any way," Stephe said. "If someone snaps at me or rags on me, I just cut 'em dead. You can say what you need to say, you just have to be respectful about it or I'll walk."

"I'm the same way. I have these friends, they've been a couple for like fifteen years, and all they do is bicker and rag on each other. It's like *Who's Afraid of Virginia Woolf* over there. Somehow it works for them but I could never be a part of something like that. "

Stephe's Muon buzzed. He got out his screen; it was Nona.

"That's my BFF Nona. I'll talk to her later."

"You can if you want, I'm comfortable here."

"Naw, it's okay. We're supposed to have lunch today."

"I was going to ask you to lunch. How about dinner tonight?"

Stephe was thrilled Max wanted to see him again so soon. He thought he could be in love.

Stephe said goodbye to Max, an adorable cowlick in his gray hair as he left, unshowered, looking up at Stephe and walking backwards for a second down the hill. They waved goodbye.

Lunch with Nona was to be at noon in the Western Addition, where she was living with Joe in a new high-rise. They met at Steak & Eggs at Fell and Octavia.

"Joe asked me to marry him!" Nona said, sitting down and pulling up her chair. She dramatically proffered her hand with a ring and tiny diamond.

"Congratulations!" Stephe kissed her on the hand and oohed and aahed over the tiny diamond chip.

"No one can afford anything during a Depression, so he apologized for the diamond, but I think it's lovely. I can't stop looking at it."

Joe was an artist—a painter, doing mad landscapes and abstract art that, frankly, Stephe couldn't understand, but his paintings sold well even during the Depression. Someone always had money. He was prolific, and his paintings didn't sell for much, but his work kept the lights on and enough food on the table. For now.

"I feel so grown-up," Nona said. "But it's really good with Joe; I like him. It's important to be able to say that. I like him."

"I met someone I quite like. I think this could be good. His name's Max; he's gorgeous and very intelligent."

"Good for you!"

"He spent the night last night. It was heavenly."

"Yay! What's he do?"

"He's an interior decorator by passion, but works for the Secretary of State in the Registrar of Voters department. He has his work cut out for him."

Stephe and Max continued to see each other any chance they could, spending every night together, either at Max's place in Dogpatch or at 472 Liberty Street.

The real reason Stephe had always remained a bachelor was he couldn't handle the idea of a gay open relationship. Yet he couldn't see himself being monogamous for very long. Gay men got used to hooking up; it's just how things were. Even though Stephe didn't consider himself to be much of a slut, preferring to have an attraction to a man before hooking up with him, he nevertheless knew he had needs and couldn't imagine a man who would meet all of them. Until he met Max. Max was it.

But Max was really hot. And fourteen years older. He was sure to have had plenty of "history," and Stephe wasn't sure he could take it. He could feel the beginnings of his jealousy even as he grappled with his own feelings. He could see being monogamous with Max—for quite a while, at least—but what would Max want? Would he demand an open relationship? Probably. Stephe was sure of it. He could tell he'd be bloody possessive of Max and that was going to be a problem.

He was going to have to get over his jealousy, and he wasn't sure he could. Jealousy was part of him, something primal and deep and was who he was. How do you surgically remove part of your own psychological make-up? It wasn't doing him any good.

Early on, he got his first test. They'd go out to the Lone Star Saloon—now in its third location at Howard Street at 9th. It had none of the charm of the old Lone Star, being on the ground floor of an aluminum-framed mid-rise condo building. But it was a good place to hang out, drink beer, play pool, listen to old rock music. Sunday beer busts were when it was really busy and the place to be. They'd socialize and meet each other's friends, and Stephe would feel jealousy when he'd encounter someone Max had slept with in the past. People blab. They don't keep secrets.

It turned Stephe's stomach. He knew Max wasn't a virgin, of course. But one guy came up and asked when Max would let him suck his dick again. He actually asked, ignoring Stephe completely. It was this sort of incursion

Stephe was going to have to get used to if he wanted to be with Max. And he did want to be with Max.

One friend of Max's, Bryce, was mildly intriguing to Stephe; tall and slender with glasses and a hooked nose and crooked smile. He and Max had obviously hooked up many times and, in his beer haze, Stephe thought it sounded like a good idea. He was calm about it this time. Bryce had a certain charm, although he seemed like kind of a slut. They joked about having a three-way and the idea wasn't nearly as horrifying to Stephe as it should have been.

Two days later Stephe was on his way to Max's with groceries; he got off the streetcar and texted Max that he was on his way.

"Bryce is here," Max wrote.

Stephe froze. Heart racing. *Shit.*

Should he leave? Not even try to go in? What would he find? Steeling himself for anything, he buzzed the door to Max's apartment building and took the elevator up to the sixth floor. He knocked, then opened the front door—it was unlocked—and there they were: Max and Bryce, dicks out, Bryce with a lascivious leer and horniness to his face; Max looked stricken, afraid.

"Hey." Stephe said as calmly as he could. "I'd better put these groceries away."

He went into the kitchen, heart pounding wildly in his chest. He could feel his own pulse in his temples. He was sick to his stomach. Face red. What was he going to do?

He was going to put away the groceries, that's what he was going to do.

He was glad to be alone in the kitchen those few seconds, figuring out his next move. He wanted to flee; he wanted to go, to keep going and never come back.

But . . . he loved Max and he liked Bryce. He loved three-ways, they were his favorite. They'd talked about it just a couple of days ago.

So what was the problem?

Stephe was at the breaking point. If he left, he'd never be back. He thrilled with anger. It was an ambush.

He forced himself to calm down.

Really, what was the big deal? He knew he needed to grow up.

Shit. The groceries were all put away, now he was just standing there in the tiny gray kitchen trying to decide what his life was going to be like, and he had about thirty seconds to choose.

Steeling himself he walked back to the couch and grabbed Bryce's penis with his left hand and bent down and kissed Max on the sofa.

They moved into the bedroom and had a damned nice three-way, very relaxing and fun, with conversation and making out and laughing. He saw Max enjoying Bryce and it actually made him feel better. It was a good, positive experience.

But Stephe knew he had a long way to go before he would lose his possessiveness over Max.

Nona was somewhat of a help later; although she was engaged to a man and didn't know the intricacies of gay relationships, she certainly understood where Stephe was coming from.

"I don't know that I believe in monogamy for straight or gay people," she said when they met for coffee a couple of days after the Bryce incident. "I'm monogamous to Joe because I like him. But what about ten years from now? I just don't think monogamy is natural."

"So what would you do," Stephe asked, "if you found out Joe was sleeping with someone else right now?"

"Oh, I'd kill him," Nona said quickly. "But that's because we're still new. Like you and Max. Ten years from now, who can say?"

"I'd be willing to be monogamous with Max if he asked me to. But he hasn't asked—we aren't really even boyfriends yet."

"Well, do that first. Sign him up as a boyfriend, if he's interested, and then you can set ground rules and sort all this out. It sounds like he really likes you."

"I think he does. I'm going to ask him if he'll be my boyfriend for a while."

"Good! Then you can work out the specifics later. Go get that puppy!"

He decided to pop the boyfriend question to Max on Friday night, at happy hour.

Probably not the best place to do it, but Stephe was anxious to get it over with. They were in a crowd at the Midnight Sun, sitting at the bar, and, heart in his throat, Stephe asked Max if he would be his boyfriend for a while.

Max grabbed his hand and said, "Thank you."

But he didn't say yes.

Next they had an art opening to go to; a friend and former fuck-buddy of Max had his work on display and they'd promised to attend. Stephe was near tears, but he went and did his best to enjoy the show. He interacted with Max as a friend, determined to keep a brave face.

But it wasn't going to be.

He went home alone that night and texted Nona:

"He didn't say yes, which means the answer is 'no.'"

Ah, well. They'd had some fun. It was definitely one for the books, as Stephe wrote in his journal. Hopefully they could still be friends; preferably friends with benefits.

The next day, Saturday, he stayed home from work, heart heavy, but no worse off than he'd always been.

Just once he wanted a real, honest-to-God boyfriend. It didn't seem to him that he was asking too much of the universe. He really wanted it to be Max.

About four o'clock he got a telephone call on his Muon. It was Max.

"How are you?"

"Good. You?"

"Fine, thanks. Say. I wanted to get back to that thing you were asking me last night."

"Yes?"

"I wasn't really tracking what you were saying. I'm sorry I didn't give you an answer. I don't know what I was thinking. The truth is I'd love to be boyfriends with you!"

Stephe was in shock. But he was relieved and delighted.

"Thanks! I think we could have fun."

"I think so, too. Do you want to come over for dinner tonight?"

"Sure!"

Stephe did so, took the Prius down to 3rd Street and was met at the door by Max and a big kiss. They had steaks, cooked on the gas grill on Max's sixth floor terrace. Max put his apartment keys on Stephe's Muon, and Stephe put the keys to 472 Liberty on Max's.

They were officially boyfriends.

But soon afterwards it was time for the "conversation."

"I have a big problem," Stephe began. "I've never had a boyfriend before. So I don't know how to handle jealousy, and it's sure to come up 'cause you're so hot. It's going to be hard for me, knowing you're still out there doing other guys. I'm not saying you can't, I just really don't want to know about it. Can you help me with that?"

"Sure. I get jealous, too."

"You do?"

"Of course I do! I'd also ask the same of you."

"So we can be a form of 'Don't Ask, Don't Tell?'"

"Yes," Max agreed. They hugged it out.

Stephe was relieved that at least Max was willing to hide his activities. That would really help. He didn't ask him for monogamy; he didn't want to be told "no" on such a sensitive question.

They dated, seriously, after that, always sleeping together either at Max's on 3rd Street, or at 472. It became comfortable. It became good.

But Stephe was always on the lookout for "Fuck Signs;" any little evidence that Max was playing around with others. The lube moved, a cockring out of place, a sex towel in the washer. He hated it when he'd find it. And he did find it. Max was still having sex outside the relationship and each little bit of evidence was like a slug to the gut. But he didn't say anything.

He had sex with Al, just to see what it was like. It was as if they were old friends, nothing more. Stephe only felt a little bit guilty. He had the power to hook up just as Max did, but there weren't any men around that could replace Max.

It was dirty work, being a gay man in a relationship. Stephe was determined to power through it. To become stronger. He worked toward the goal of having mastery over his jealousy. Some day, he'd get there.

Max was a mountain of a man, snored, had a CPAP machine so he slept with his mask on and Stephe got used to the idea, fell asleep every night to the quiet hum of the machine.

Nona got married to Joe in 2035 and Stephe was Maid of Honor. It was a simple ceremony at Mission Dolores; Nona's father Francisco walked Nona down the aisle when he got to Joe, he shook his hand.

The wedding reception was a blast. Natalie was there. Stephe brought Max, André from Berkeley and Nicole from work. Everyone was delightfully sloshed and Stephe was very proud of Nona. She chose well with Joe—they looked like an excellent couple together.

Stephe was proud to dance with Nona in her wedding dress. She was right; it felt very grown-up.

In November of 2035 Stephe decided to throw a Thanksgiving dinner. Although his cooking was pretty adequate he was nervous about doing a turkey with all the trimmings for seven people. The groceries cost over $1,400.

The guests were to be him and Max, Margery, Jack and Elena, Nona and Joe. A dinner party for seven. Max helped; he was a great cook. Max was in charge of the vegetables, sweet potatoes and the gravy.

Stephe spent two days getting ready, reading up on how to cook a turkey and dressing.

The guests began arriving at two o'clock: Elena, Nona and Joe. Nona and Joe brought Brinkman, a chow-boxer mix, quite possibly the cutest dog in existence.

Margery made the mashed potatoes.

Jack had grown into a very All-American look, tall, blond, athletic. Very straight but still cool.

Elena had long brown hair and what Stephe supposed was a good figure—he wasn't one to judge—and she was a CPA in Oakland.

Joe was tall, dark and brooding; average looks but a twinkle in his eye, very bright but shy, not one for extraneous conversation.

Everyone except Margery tucked into the wine heartily. It became raucous over the dinner table. They'd kind of discussed not being too screamingly liberal in front of Margery so as to not offend her conservative sensibilities. But after so much wine and food, the agreement was forgotten. Politics came up.

"They say the U.S. dollar is now worth fifteen cents compared to 2020."

"Collapse of the U.S., and they've still got most of the nukes."

"No drinking water in North Carolina."

Max tended to get bombastic when he drank. He launched into the voter fraud situation and was able to fill in many of the blanks surrounding the problems with voting: "The Muon Spoof was the biggest crime of the century. And everybody knows it," he said. "Several states are considering returning to paper balloting after the past few elections; but, since the people in power are the ones winning, it's an uphill fight. History is written by the winners."

Margery remained silent and prim, not participating in the conversation.

Finally she interjected. "I actually have some big news," she said. Everyone turned to look at her. "Come to find out, I've decided to take my retirement and return to Colorado; to Fort Collins."

Stephe was stunned.

Jack said, "Margery, you can't be serious! Fort Collins is outside the Denver Bubble. You want to live in the U.S. again?"

"Indeed I do!" she replied. "Things are much too expensive here in California; they tax you on everything. It's all Big Government. I think the U.S. would be a much better fit for me."

A pall was cast over the table.

"Margery," Jack said, "of course we support you, no matter what you choose, but we'll *miss* you!"

"Yeah," Stephe added, still in shock. "This place wouldn't be the same without you. Are you sure you want to leave?"

"I'll miss you guys too," she responded, "but my mind is made up. Actually I'm so excited about retiring it's all I can think of."

"Ms. Johnson," Nona said, "I'm so happy for you. Congratulations on reaching retirement. That's huge! I know how long and hard you've worked over the years; you've been a great help around here. I can't imagine this house without you in it!"

Good old Nona. Always knew the perfect thing to say.

"I'll miss it here, I'll miss this house and you two boys more than I can say. But it's time to move on."

"When does this happen?" Stephe asked.

"I'm thinking in January," Margery answered.

Christmas 2035 came and went; very subdued with the news of Margery's departure. Stephe and Max made a Christmas dinner with the exact same guest list as Thanksgiving and it went off without a hitch. It was warm and cozy; the windows fogged up and Christmas lights were always important to Stephe so there were many strands hung about.

On January 14, 2036, Margery moved back to Fort Collins, Colorado. She had come with two suitcases and she left with the same ones. Most of the same clothes, too; Margery didn't have much to do with clothes and wardrobes.

It was a sad day for Jack and Stephe; Margery seemed rather jubilant.

The Uber was waiting; it was time to go.

"Margery, thank you for all you've done. We couldn't have made it without you!" Stephe gave her a huge hug—she held herself stiffly and thumped his back.

"I wouldn't have had it any other way," she said. "I was glad I could be here for you."

"Call us when you get where you're going, okay?" said Jack, giving her a hug as well.

And with that she crawled into her Uber and was off.

"End of an era," Jack said sadly.

"I hope she finds happiness," answered Stephe.

Chapter 18

In January 2036, Alabama was the first state to outlaw homosexuality by legislative decree, signed by the governor.

The ruling was quickly followed by Arkansas, Tennessee and Mississippi.

Hundreds of gays, lesbians and transgendered people were arrested, roughed up and jailed. The states didn't know what to do with them—they couldn't get caught killing them—so camps were set up at taxpayer expense. The prison systems had been private since the Trump years; there was a lot of money to be made.

At first few people were arrested—no one wanted to actually go there—but soon came reports of beatings and arrests and rumors of mass lynchings.

So people by the thousands began to flee to safer states: Georgia, Florida, North and South Carolina and Texas, where gay rights were no longer guaranteed, but at least it wasn't illegal—yet.

They flocked to Atlanta, overwhelming the city.

Stephe was sent to Atlanta in February for three days to interview refugees, accompanied by Duane, the top archivist for The Gay Liberation Front. They met at SFO and flew on Delta, on a Boeing 808, from The California Republic to Atlanta and cleared customs. They were both nervous as hell.

They were hosted by a gay couple in Midtown, Eric and Eric, in a swell apartment with a terrier and a terrace.

Stephe managed a telephone interview with Atlanta Mayor Wallace.

"Is your city welcoming to gay people?" Stephe inquired.

"We don't don't have room for everybody," Wallace responded. "We're not a full-blown Autonomous City Region. We're still part of Georgia as a whole. So there are no borders here. We're being overwhelmed."

"People say that homosexuality will be outlawed in Georgia as well."

"That bill is in the state House as we speak."

"What will life be like in Atlanta for gay people if the bill is enacted?"

"Well, we'll have to follow state law," Wallace replied.

"So, no protection for lesbians and gay men?"

"Not in the eyes of the law," Wallace concluded.

The Phillip Rush Center on DeKalb Avenue was the main Gay and Lesbian Center for the Atlanta area. With permission from the head director, Stephe and Duane set about interviewing refugees. Allison was their liaison, head of the legal department at the Rush Center. She had arranged three interviews for the day.

The first, Skyler, told his story to Stephe and Duane. Thin, a young man of twenty-eight, hair in a purple wave on top:

I was living in an apartment with my boyfriend, Mark, in Birmingham, Alabama. Of course we'd rather have lived here in Atlanta, but who can afford it? Apartments here are $35,000 a month, and that's if you're lucky. Still, we were pretty content, kept a low profile. Our neighbors were cool—or so we thought. One night last month, the neo-Nazis came through the neighborhood with torches, and they beat up some black people and spray-painted all the cars. They broke car windows, apartment windows— anything that could break.

Our apartment was on the ground floor so they smashed out our living room windows and threw in a Molotov cocktail, which we were able, thank God, to put out with a pot of hot spaghetti water before it blew up. They spray-painted "FAG" all over our front door and outer walls and our car. We hid in the bathroom, then, until it was over. The police came but didn't do anything. Some people were beaten pretty badly; they got ambulances for them but just took statements and left.

When we called the landlord to tell him of the damages, he yelled at us like it was our fault. He said he wouldn't fix anything and expected us to repaint and fix our own windows. I was in shock; Mark was furious. He said he'd contact the state rent board. He said he'd paint the outside of the apartment bright pink and *leave* it there. But we needed windows right away. It was cold. The first three contractors we called, when they saw the mess and the "FAG" part, wouldn't take the job. The fourth one did, but he wanted the money up front.

We limped along and got things cleared up. But on, like, Day Four the cops came and arrested us for being a public nuisance.

They wouldn't let us grab our keys or our screens; they just handcuffed us and took us away in a squad car, chained like animals.

When we got to the station we were put into different rooms and made to strip to our under-wear—it was damn cold in there and they never offered us a towel or blanket.

They kept asking about our relationship, who did what to whom. They asked all these intimate, sexual questions. At first I didn't answer anything, but they just kept wearing me down, wearing me down. I was weak from the cold and hunger and finally started snarling answers at them: "Three years we've been together, I'm a bottom he cums in me with his fat black dick and I like it!"

One of the cops gave me a backhand smack, right across the mouth. It was so strong it took my breath away, and, still being handcuffed, I flew out of my chair and hit the floor. They picked me back up and sat me back down. I was woozy.

After a while of this, writing down everything I said, they put me in an orange jumpsuit and stuck me in a cell with three other guys—gang-bangers, real criminals, and here's me, a tiny gay thing with a puffy face and a fat lip. I was also the only white guy.

One of the guys in the cell just pointed to one of the lower, empty bunks and I lay down on it and curled up in a ball. I ignored them and they ignored me, but it was unnerving, hearing all the sounds and shouts and cat calls echoing around the cell block. I thought about yelling out for Mark, in case he was somewhere in there, too, but knew it wouldn't come off right with my cell mates.

It was at night that I was awoken to a hand over my mouth and a ripping-open of my jumpsuit. I was in a full body lock while the other guy ripped off my jumpsuit and pulled it down around my ankles.

Stephe swallowed, sick at what was to come next.

Skyler said, "They both did it; took turns, one guy holding me down while the other one finished his business, and then they traded places."

Skyler paused, his eyes teared up. "Something so joyous can practically be a murder weapon. I wanted to die. I've never felt so horrible, so ashamed, so hurt in my life. It was disgusting and terrifying. I still have to remind myself: I've been gang-raped in jail. I feel so dirty."

"I'm so sorry," Duane interjected. "Do you need to stop?"

"No, I'm all right," Skyler answered. Then he continued:

That was the only time they came at me; I don't even know which two it was...well, I knew one of them, I could tell by the way he smelled and by his skin. So they just did it once, sort of a "Welcome to the Neighborhood." But of course I didn't know it was just going to be once. I was coiled up tense as a spring, waiting for another assault. Thank God none came.

It was all I could do to stay sane.

Finally, we got set before a judge: fifteen of us at once. Mark was there, but we could only make eye contact. They made it look like a trial, but it wasn't. Someone, a lawyer from the Gay Liberation Front, was there and pleaded our case, but the judge didn't listen. Still, this judge was nice. Nicer than he could have been. He fined us each one point five million

and let us go for time served and two years proba-
tion. But we'd be registered as sex offenders. We'd
be monitored by Muon and couldn't leave Alabama.
He cautioned us against ever appearing in his court
again—by which he meant we'd better not be caught
being gay again.

"What did you do then?" Stephe asked.
Skyler continued:

Well, it took them a while to process us back
out, give us our clothes back. Take the handcuffs off.
Of course, Mark and I ran to each other and were
hugging when one of the cops cracked me over the
head with his nightstick. Christ, that hurt! I nearly
blacked out, but we parted and acted like strangers
to each other until we got out of there.

We met in the park across the street; it was cold
and we didn't have jackets or screens.

I didn't want to even go back to the apartment
to get our stuff; Mark said don't be stupid, we didn't
have enough money to start over, but we actually
did. I had quite a bit stashed in savings I'd never told
him about. We talked about just leaving, coming to
Georgia. Yes, we'd be Muoned the minute we crossed
the border, but would the Georgia police hand us back
to Alabama for being gay? It's still legal in Georgia,
although not by much. We decided to chance it.

We Ubered back to our apartment anyway. I was
nervous; I'd had money in my account, but what if it
was gone? But charge for the Uber ride went through
okay.

Our car was burnt. The apartment had been

ransacked; defiled. Graffitied. Everything of value was gone, our screens and appliances; everything else thrown around. But we each grabbed a coat and a few small items and left. Never to go back.

We stopped by an AT&T store to buy screens for our Muons—cheap ones—and got food at a diner. I had enough money to rent a car, wondering if we'd be flagged as felons or something but it was okay. The girl at the car rental place was nice. We were starting to feel normal again.

We rode to the border and drove across on I-20 and the minute we crossed into Georgia, sure enough, our screens lit up that we were in violation of our parole and subject to arrest. We figured they were just bluffing, and in a way they were; there was no extradition situation set in place. We just rode all the way into Atlanta and straight to the car rental place to get rid of the car. We came here to the Rush Center and basically turned ourselves in. They were very helpful and found us a room to stay at; there've been a lot of refugees from Alabama and they kinda have a network in place.

The problem is getting jobs. We're felons, and sex offenders, according to our Muons, and that shit stays with you no matter where you go. Mark got a job waiting tables at a gay café in Midtown, and I have an interview next week at a gay-owned software company. I sure hope I get it. Things are getting tight and we want to move out from where we're staying—they've been great but we've imposed long enough.

Next they interviewed Valerie, a lesbian in her early forties:

We were living in Little Rock, Arkansas, my lover Sonya and I. We were constantly being harassed by our neighbors: Proud Boys. Sonya wanted to move but I stood my ground. One day, though, walking our dog one late afternoon, we got beat up in the street. That convinced me to finally move.

We got a small place in Sweet Home, and it was much quieter—a cute little house with a garden—but a neighbor turned us in. We got arrested, processed, and put in jail. We were eventually released with a warning. We got out of jail and beat feet straight to Atlanta. On the bus. We thought about cutting our Muons out of our wrists—people did that—but it left you pretty stuck; there's not much you can do without one.

While in Atlanta there was a demonstration in Midtown—the Gay Pride March—and Freedom Fighters showed up and violence broke out. Tear gas, bludgeonings. The cops protected the Freedom Fighters, not the lesbians and gays.

Shots rang out from somewhere and Sonya went down. She took a bullet to the stomach. She died in the hospital. They wouldn't let me be with her, they just left me sobbing in the hall until they finally told me to leave.

By far the most nauseating and frightful account came from a man named Jaden:

It was about two weeks ago. Four of us were in a car coming back from a gay bar in Jackson, Mississippi. Club Rain. It was about ten o'clock at night on a Saturday. Some yahoos in two different pick-up trucks followed us and tried running us off the road. I was in the car with Dylan Jones, Mike Miller, and Kyle Milton; I was driving. It turned into a chase, I floored it and tried to outrun them but these guys had heavy-duty trucks and here's me in a Honda hybrid. We didn't have a chance. I shouldn't have done it, but I turned out Old Brandon Road, heading away from the city to the southeast. I'm still kicking myself. It was a big mistake. I turned onto a side road—an even bigger mistake. I could kill myself.

They finally ran us into a ditch halfway out toward Pearl. There was no one around. We were banged up in the ditch, the car at a crazy angle. We locked the doors as the bubbas jumped out of their pickups and surrounded my car. They tried the door handles, when that didn't work they smashed out the windows and started pistol-whipping us with their guns. They had knives. They cut Kyle and Mike out of their seatbelts and dragged 'em from the car and started beating them, laughing, calling them "fucking faggots." There were five of them and four of us and they had guns and knives. Two of them broke away to cut me and Dylan out—we were at the lower side of the car, our doors wouldn't open, being half turned over in the ditch; we kicked and fought them off as best we could, but these were big guys. Two of them got together and dragged Dylan up and out of the back seat and threw him onto the ground. Then they came for me.

I hung onto the steering wheel as tight as I could,

but one of them bashed my hand with the butt of his gun and I had to let go. They pulled me out and threw me on top of Dylan on the ground.

They got rope from a truck and tied me and Dylan together face to face in a freakish hug position. I though Mike and Kyle were unconscious, I could barely make them out lying on the ground a few feet away. It was so dark.

They tied up Mike and Kyle separately, hands behind their backs. The were still conscious after all; they kicked and tried to fight.

"Let's have some fun," one of them said. They grabbed Kyle and threw him over the hood of my car and pulled his pants down and . . . "

Jaden stopped. He let out a jagged sigh.

They took turns on him, one after the other. All five of them.

We were yelling for help but each time we'd get smacked upside the head. Hard. I didn't know how much that could hurt. We were reeling from the pain.

The last guy mounted Kyle and, still inside him, pulled out his gun and shot Kyle in the head. He just let him fall to the ground, pants around his legs, head half gone.

That's when we lost it. We all started screaming and fighting against our ropes and it was like the bubbas got the smell of blood, they started kicking us and beating us. I heard another gunshot—it doesn't sound like it does in the movies, it's more of a "snap!" sound—and I knew another one of us was gone. It was Mike. Face down on the ground, hands still tied behind his back.

That left Dylan and me, tied face to face.

It was so dark I couldn't even make out his face. But I knew we were going to die. We leaned into each other not knowing what to say. Hearts pounding in terror.

Just then a car came by, I don't know why I remember, but it was a white Kia, I could tell by the headlights; the car seemed to slow a little. A brief moment of hope, dashed. The car roared off.

"We should get the fuck outta here," one of the men said and three jumped into one of the pickups. I thought me and Dylan were going to be okay and as the last of the two men turned to leave, one of them raised his gun sideways and blew Dylan away. He crumpled to the ground, taking me with him, and I heard the last two men jump into their truck and they all sped off.

And so there I was. On the ground, tied to a dead and bleeding body—someone who'd been my friend for years; we even went out a few times before. I could just lay there in the cold with Dylan. I couldn't wrap my head around what just happened, it all made no sense. I had wet myself.

It was cold and getting colder. Dylan grew cooler to the touch; I could tell I was covered in his coagulating blood. There was nothing to do. So I did what I could to fiddle with the knots in the rope tying us together. My hands were bent to the breaking point but I could loosen one of the cords. I spent a good two hours that way, loosening the ropes a fraction of an inch at a time until finally one of the knots came undone. That made it a little easier to get to the next one.

Finally, after about three hours, I was free of the knots, but the rope was still wound around the both of us, and Dylan was heavy. All that work and I still couldn't free my arms. I was freezing by then. Dylan's body pulled the heat from my own. I still had to try. Apologizing to Dylan I kicked us around, rolling us and unspooling the rope. It was incredibly hard work. His body was becoming stiff. After the first circuit I could use my right arm a little, got more leverage, and kept rolling us until my right arm was a little freer.

After all that I was able to reach the screen in my pocket and call 9-1-1.

The cops got there first. "Jesus," was all they'd say. By the time the ambulance was there the cops had cut me free from Dylan and sat me in the front seat of the squad car with the heat on. I was so bloody they had to put a blanket down first. They scanned my Muon, saw the drinks receipts from Club Rain, so they drove me to the police station and arrested me for being gay.

My mom came and bailed me out. They'd fished my car out of the ditch. It was in the impound lot, banged up with broken windows and cut up seatbelts, but it still ran. I didn't even tell my mom I was going, I just got on the road. I had to choose between Austin ACR or Atlanta; I have a sister here in Atlanta so I chose to come here. Maybe not the wisest choice, considering what's been going on now. I've been staying with my sister and her girlfriend, sleeping on the couch. Finally called my mom to let her know I was safe. The Rush Center hooked me up with a counselor.

Jaden kept wiping his palms on his jeans. He finally said, "So that's what happened."

They stood, and Stephe and Duane both gave him a hug.

"Thank you for your story," Duane said. "I know this must have been hard."

"It's not good," Jaden said. "I hope things can get better, but I don't see how. They want blood now. Our blood. And that's exactly what they're going to get."

Stephe and Duane were wrung out.

Stephe wrote Jaden's story, published it to *Equality Magazine,* and pronounced that he needed a drink. Their hosts, Eric and Eric, took them out to dinner in Midtown, at a place called Enoteca—a swanky Italian bistro with gay waiters buzzing around in tight black pants and a huge wine list. Stephe and Duane got a little tipsy, sort of a release from the horrors of the day. It felt normal, like being in San Francisco.

He got a call from Max that night. "I just read your article. Jesus!"

"Yeah. This is bad. And it's happening all over the South. Atlanta's bursting at the seams. I think something big is going to happen."

"Sounds like it. I worry about you."

"Oh, I'll be all right. I'm surrounded by homosexuals and people here are surprisingly upbeat."

"Atlanta isn't a Bubble City, is it?" Max asked. They'd already had this conversation before Stephe left.

"No, technically it's not. It's still part of Georgia; so if Georgia goes, the whole place goes with it."

"Well I'll feel a hell of a lot better when you're back home in California."

"Me, too," Stephe answered.

"Anyway, I know it's a day early, but Happy Birthday to you for tomorrow!"

"Thanks! I can't believe I'm going to be twenty-nine."

"I still can't believe I'm dating a twenty-nine-year-old. I feel like such an old man."

"You're sexy as hell. Can't wait to see you when I get back."

"Well, happy birthday tomorrow. I love you," Max said warmly.

"I love you, too. G'night."

"G'night."

The next day at the Rush Center, Stephe was to interview staff and learn of the networks in place to house all the refugees coming to Atlanta. Duane was to continue the horrible task of interviewing refugees for the archives. Stephe was relieved his day wouldn't be as enervating as the day before. They were sitting in the open floor plan, desks all around, on the couches, having a relaxing day. Except for Duane, seated in a conference room, hearing more tales of doom.

Suddenly the news tweeted in on everyone's Muon at the same time: Homosexuality was now illegal in Georgia.

Everyone went silent.

A girl cried.

A delivery man loudly burst in just then with a bouquet of roses.

"Flowers for a Stephe Stafford?" he said, clearly puzzled by the tense silence in the room.

"Here," Stephe said eventually, getting off the couch to take the roses. The card read "Happy Birthday, Stephe; love, Max." Stephe Muoned the guy $300 and the man said "Thank you!" And as he walked away toward the door he spoke a word so softly it took Stephe several seconds to decipher what it was:

"Fags."

Everyone emptied into the streets of Atlanta. It became a tidal wave. Every gay man and lesbian woman, every transgendered person, every concerned, supportive citizen poured into the streets. People walked off their jobs and took to the sidewalks. Midtown shut down.

On a pre-arranged signal, every man and woman on the sidewalk wended their way into the streets and sat down.

The city was paralyzed.

Half the Atlanta Police Force sat down as well.

Cars couldn't move. Soon the cacophony of a thousand car horns blared into the afternoon air; deafening. In a few cases cars inched forward, causing protestors to crab-walk out of their way, only to be met with more sitting protesters a few feet on. There were thousands.

Eventually the horns stopped. Some people abandoned their cars and joined the protesters, or stomped off in a huff.

For four hours not a soul moved. There were no chants, no signs, no violence: Only silence.

News drones buzzed overhead, sending their feeds to all the major news services—even Fox News got in on the reporting.

When the four hours were over, stiff and sore and needing to pee, the protesters scraped themselves from off the streets and went back to their lives.

It was a warning: Mess with us and we'll cripple you.

Georgia Governor Wendy Clark and Atlanta Mayor Wallace messed with them anyway.

Arrests began the next day.

The police stormed the Philip Rush Center first and cracked heads and arrested Stephe, Duane, Allison and everyone else. For the second time in his life, Stephe was arrested. They were thrown into a van and driven to police headquarters, where hundreds of gay men and women waited in vans, in the halls, in rooms. Muons scanned. Stephe was separated from Duane and the others—he was on his own with fifty other people in a courtroom, all defendants, sentenced en masse to the crime of homosexuality. Several people were beaned on the head with nightsticks. Screens confiscated.

After sentencing they were driven away in police vans. They kept it beastly hot in the van, Stephe fought to keep from passing out. A little old woman sat next to him weeping. Stephe asked if she was okay.

"Of *course* I'm not okay! *None* of this is okay!"

"I know." He held her hand and she wept less.

"My name's Stephe," he said softly.

"I'm Enid," she responded. "I got separated from my lover, Iris; she's quite a bit older. I don't know what happened to her. She's been so frail lately."

"I'm sorry! Maybe you'll find her when we get where we're going."

"Where *are* we going? Looks like Decatur."

They pulled into the parking lot of a huge warehouse.

Georgia State Patrol vehicles everywhere.

There was a processing building, where everyone was checked in, Muoned again. Most personal effects were taken.

"Who's paying for all this?" Enid moaned.

"You are, sweetheart," said one of the guards lightly.

Finally they were led through the building and put into caged sections, just like the children of immigrants back in the early days of the Trump Administration. Hundreds of people were milling around, sitting in their cages. About half were still in civilian clothes. Enid found Iris, her lover.

Stephe was assigned Space 1806 and went and lay on the only unoccupied cot. Men and women were mixed, many more men than women; a few straight gang-bangers and liberals and larcenists. There were twelve to a cage, cots shoved next to one another.

He waited. There was nothing else to do.

Finally, on the third day, Stephe got assigned a work detail. From 7 a.m. to 7 p.m. doing construction on a large apartment complex down the road. Food was provided. It wasn't good, but it beat having nothing.

Every morning at six, Stephe and the others were awoken. His day would start with coffee and toast in a section of the warehouse dubbed "the mess hall." It was a wave of people pushing and shoving for toast and bad coffee. Then they, in their orange jumpsuits, would be assigned a van and taken to a construction site. As a gay man and a prisoner, there wasn't a lot for Stephe to do; they weren't allowed anywhere near the power tools for obvious reasons. He was often just in charge of stacking bricks, clearing out lumber debris, and working with the straight and very disdainful contractors, holding boards for measurements and putting joists in place so they could be hammered in. He wasn't very good at it, but it was better than a lot of assignments he'd heard of—actual digging of ditches and hauling of cement.

One of the construction foremen was really hot but a withering asshole. Stephe's Muon went *Click!* every time he had to interact with the man and it made him sick to his stomach. No way to shut it off.

They'd be given a sandwich and a Coke at noon, and then the van would come back at seven to take him and the four others back to the warehouse. Dinner in the mess hall was usually a TV dinner, chicken and peas.

It was bleak. He had no hope of getting out of there, no way of letting Max know where he was—oh, how he missed Max! Did Max miss him, too? Or would he have moved on, picking up Bryce or some skinny chick and just moving on with his life? Stephe agonized over it.

He was in hell.

Chapter 19

On Day Eight, Stephe was liberated.

It ended with the Gay Liberation Front bailing Stephe out because he was a Californian and a journalist.

A terse sergeant came and got him from the breakfast table and told him to report to the warden's office. Sensing he was in trouble, he was horrified as he made his way to the main office at one end of the building. After waiting for an hour, wondering if he was going to be in further trouble for missing work, he was brought before an official at a desk who told him he was being released.

"You're a Californian, which means the powers that be say you're immune from prosecution in Georgia. Here's your shit. You're advised to get on a plane and not come back."

Stephe was elated. They gave him his clothes and his screen and he changed, buck naked, right there in front of the warden or whoever he was. They escorted him out, through a series of gates, and dumped him out on Scott Road in Decatur.

Stephe was surprised that his money was still in his account. He called an Uber and one came in about ten minutes. While he was waiting he called Max.

"Oh my God, I'm so glad to see you!" Max looked distraught. "Are you okay?"

"I'm okay, yeah, I guess. They let me go."

"They damn well better have! I spent every day at the Gay Liberation Front offices. Their lawyers worked their asses off to get you out of there!"

"Thank you! I'm so relieved!"

"Was it bad?"

"Yeah. They didn't beat me, but they did beat others; you can't speak up or complain, you have to work. They had me on a construction site for twelve hours a day."

"Shit. You look like you've lost weight. Where are you now?"

"I'm outside the prison waiting for my Uber. I'm going straight to the airport, I'm not even going to go back to get my stuff at my host's apartment. God knows if they're even still there."

"They probably aren't. Do you need money for the plane ticket?" Max asked.

"No, I think I'll be fine, even for a last-minute one-way ticket. I should be good."

"Well, let me know what flight you're on and I'll come get you."

"Goddamn, that would be sweet. Thank you!"

"No problem! That's what boyfriends are for. I'll see you in a couple of hours."

By this time his Uber was pulling up and Stephe got in the back seat.

"Thanks, Max! I'll see you soon!"

"I love you."

"I love you, too!"

"Hell of a place to need a ride," the Uber driver, a woman, said.

"Yeah, not my first choice."

"So you were inside? What's it like?" she asked, looking in the rearview mirror.

"Not good. They fed us, made us work. Couple of beatings."

"I hear people 'disappear,'" and she made air quotes before folding her hands politely in her lap as the car drove itself.

"Some people have gone missing; we don't know if they got extradited, transferred or shot."

"Goddamn," she said. "It's a hell of a world gone mad. I just don't get it."

They went straight to Atlanta Hartsfield International Airport and it cost Stephe $2100 for the Uber and $31,000 for a one-way flight to San Francisco.

He was flooded with relief when he Muoned onto the plane and no one stopped him. He splurged on an inflight snack box and a double scotch and landed in foggy cool San Francisco an hour and a half later.

He got held up in Customs and Immigration. He was asked a lot of questions about his prison time in Georgia, but he got the impression they were more curious than concerned. They let him go.

Max was waiting for him with flowers outside of Customs. So was Nicole and his boss David—and several television newscasters. Hugs all around and a big wet kiss from Max. As always, Stephe still had to put one foot back to keep from losing his balance when kissing or hugging Max.

He stepped in front of the reporters, holding Max's hand, and answered their questions about Atlanta and the detention facility as best he could.

"What was it like?"

"Was there any mistreatment?"

Stephe answered that one: "The entire process was a dehumanizing mistreatment! I saw several people being beaten and we were forced to do labor. They took our clothes, they took our screens, and then they put us in cages."

"Did people go missing?"

"Several people disappeared," Stephe said to the CNN reporter. "We don't know what happened to them. We don't know if they were transferred . . . or executed."

"Were you allowed access to medical care?"

"No," Stephe answered, "no attempt was made to get people their prescription medications. None at all."

He was peppered with questions, but it all became repetitive after a while. The flurry of interrogatives died down and the reporters thanked him for his time, each shaking his hand. He was finally free to get out of there.

They all piled into a driverless Uber and Stephe recounted his tales and heard from David all the work they did behind the scenes getting him out of Georgia.

San Francisco. It felt so good to be home! Many times during his eight days he was sure he'd never see it again, that he'd die alone in a prison camp.

They dropped Stephe and Max off at 472 Liberty Street, and Nicole and David went on in the Uber.

"I need a bath!" Stephe said. Max volunteered to draw his bath for him. After his bath they made love and lay in bed, Max holding Stephe tight and repeating, "I'm so glad you're safe."

He could have stayed home from work the next day but he went in to applause from his co-workers and a standing ovation. He trudged to his desk and immediately began banging out his stories. He had the first one published in an hour: Arrested for being gay and put into a warehouse in Georgia. It had 142,000 "Likes" by the end of the day.

Texas was the next to go. While Stephe was in the detention facility, the Texas legislature moved from Austin ACR back to Houston, which had been the original state capitol in 1836. It then outlawed homosexuality in the state. People flocked to Austin for sanctuary in droves, many arrested en route. Similar to Georgia, Texas began housing the detainees in empty warehouses, behind chain-link fences. Thousands were incarcerated, costing the state coffers thousands of dollars per night, per prisoner, all paid for by the taxpayers.

California and the rest of the ACRs put heavy pressure on Alabama, Mississippi, Georgia, Arkansas, Tennessee and Texas to end their heinous mistreatment of gays and lesbians; even the UN New York was bearing down on those states. Boycotts and sanctions were put in place. But it fell on deaf ears. Too much money to be made.

It all began to take its toll. Stephe, by 2037, was starting to fall apart. Enough was enough. He couldn't bear to turn his back on all the suffering, but his stomach was always in knots and he drank a lot. He felt like he was shouldering the burden on his own; his counselor of course told him this wasn't true, it only felt that way.

His therapist, Beate, was a German woman in a nice house in the Richmond District. He did great work with Beate, but he was falling apart. He could tell.

"You're living through a holocaust," Beate said. "It's so bad out there and you're a witness to the entire thing, no wonder you're distraught. "

"I'm thinking of getting another job. Of turning my back on the whole thing—but then that feels so bad and callous I hate myself for thinking it."

"What have you accomplished?" Beate asked.

"Huh?"

"In your seven years there, have you accomplished anything?"

"Fuck yes!" Stephe said defensively, not sure where she was going with this.

"Well, then you've made a difference. You've made the world a better place, even if in increments. Maybe you're done; maybe it's okay if you step aside and let others take your place."

Stephe was floored. But he was also flooded with relief. He wasn't indispensable, half a dozen people could take over. Was he making a difference? Sometimes he couldn't tell. It was like sweeping back the ocean with a broom.

He left, took the B-Line back in on Geary Boulevard and headed to meet Max at Civic Center. They were going to Tu-Lan Vietnamese, on 6th Street, still there after all these years.

He was near tears when he met Max.

"Beate and I talked about my leaving the GLF."

"My God, hallelujah!"

"Do you think I should?"

"I do. I mean, I can tell how turned on you are by your job, but I can also see how it's tearing you apart. Maybe it's time to let other people into the fray?"

"That's exactly what my therapist said."

"Well? So it's true. She and I are smart people. You should obey us. Meanwhile, what are you going to have?"

Stephe ordered the same thing he always got there, the lemon beef salad over rice. Heavenly.

They went to Max's place down on 3rd. No Fuck Sign. Which was good, Stephe wasn't in the mood. They watched TCM and had wine until it was time to sleep.

The next day was a Saturday and they decided to drive out of the city and go to Guerneville. Max surprised Stephe with a night's stay at the Highland's Resort. The old town of Guerneville, nestled in the redwoods, hadn't changed much; the town had flooded out several times, it always flooded there in winter. They went to Armstrong Woods and walked among the giant Sequoias, their footfalls muted in pine needles. Sound was different in there; muffled, soft. It was like a tonic for Stephe. They ate dinner out and settled by the fire in the cabin in the woods and made love in the dark.

It wasn't logical to shuttle back and forth between Liberty Street and 3rd Street in Dogpatch to see Max every night. But Max wasn't in a hurry to live together. "That's always when bad things start happening," Max said. "I like things how they are; I like my apartment."

"I get that; it's a nice apartment and I know you like your privacy. It's just that I've got this huge house sitting there, bought and paid for; Jack has moved to Oakland with Elena and we'd have so much room. We could get a dog."

"A dog?"

"Sure! All gay men living in the Castro have to have dogs; it's the rule."

Max laughed. "I'll tell you what," he said; "I promise I'll think about it. I know that I want to be with you, so it's not that; please don't think it's that."

"I don't. I know."

"Good."

Eventually Max caved in. They decided to live together. Stephe was ecstatic. Max seemed to be, too. "I suppose we'll have to fight about little things, like how to hang the toilet paper roll."

"Oh, you mean like making sure it always hangs down the back?" Stephe joked.

"Grrrr. Never!"

"Listen, for you, I'll fold it into a little point like at a nice hotel every morning."

"Grrr."

"I know, right?"

Stephe soldiered on at work the best he could. By all reports, thousands of gay men and women were in detention centers throughout the South and no one seemed to have an answer. The GLF tried various legal tricks to extradite people, but most attempts were for naught.

Stephe even heard from Jeremy in North Carolina.

"It's really bad here," Jeremy wrote. "They love to beat up fags. I can usually pass, I don't look like a fag, but since all my friends here are gay, I'm guilty by association. It's like I can't leave the house except to go to work. They don't know I'm gay there, and I'm not going to tell 'em. All the bars have closed down, and Growlr's not safe; you don't know who you're talking to. Neo-Nazis like to infiltrate the chat boards posing as gay guys and then beat you up if you try to meet them. Hell, they record it and upload it to YouTube!"

Stephe had seen the videos. He couldn't stomach them. They were all in the archives, hundreds of them, waiting for a time when all of this would, once again, be in the past and there would be a record of when humanity, once again, took leave of its senses.

Chapter 20

Meanwhile, offworld, the population of the Moon had climbed to over a million people. Mostly the very rich. All that rock was fashioned into apartments and office buildings. Armstrong Park was built in the heart of Tayin City; a great domed Central Park for Moon residents and tourists alike. It became legendary; climate-controlled, rare tropical plants, public swimming pools and even horses, which delighted in the lower gravity.

The Moon was truly international. America had lost the space race to the Chinese, Russians and East Indians long ago. Everything was in four languages, and people communicated by Muon; it had an instant translation feature. The Lunar government was similar to that of an ACR. They had their own currency and their own news network: The LNN.

Two years after the Culture War was over, the United States settled down. The bombings stopped. Three Mile Island was still a nuclear wasteland and the Bubble Cities began thriving. Trade with the U.S. became normalized; a lot fewer people were starving to death. The Dust Bowl was over and agriculture started again—saving the U.S. the embarrassment of having to purchase food from the Russians and the Chinese.

The outlawing of homosexuality spread to a few more states in the South, but then it stopped. As profitable as it was, the push-back was huge. The following states had outlawed homosexuality: Arkansas, Alabama, Mississippi, Georgia, Texas, Tennessee and Indiana.

Chapter 21

Burned out at the GLF, Stephe started applying for other jobs. Once again, he tried the *SF Chronicle*, the local TV affiliates and, as before, managed to get a few interviews and vague promises—he was an on-screen personality as well as a reporter. But the competition was extreme.

An obscure group on LinkedIn tried to recruit him for a job similar to what he had at the GLF. Knowing nothing about what the job really was, he went on an interview. Strangely, it was to be held at a restaurant, the Top of the Mark at the Hopkins Hotel on California Street. He was met by a man named Nassir Gupta.

"Thank you for coming," Mr. Gupta said, and he invited Stephe to sit down. They exchanged pleasantries, talked about the weather, and ordered lunch. Stephe ordered a Cobb salad and iced tea.

"Our news organization is small," Nassir began, "but we're looking for someone who can handle a wide variety of news stories and sources. The job would be writing and a lot of on-screen reporting. We've been watching your vlogs and reporting for the Gay Liberation Front for some time, and we were quite pleased to see your post on LinkedIn."

"Thank you," Stephe replied.

"We have a total of five candidates we're sifting through; I wish I could give you a smaller number, but one of the five of you will be selected."

"I'm thrilled just to be considered."

"The pay is generous. It'll be a . . . prestigious . . . position. Have you a CV we can take a look at?"

Of course Stephe did; he Muoned it to Nassir.

"Thank you; we'll give it all due consideration."

The interview went the way of most interviews: "What's your worst bad habit?" "How would you handle conflicting situations?" "Where did you go to school?" It was very informal. It didn't feel that much like an interview, and since Stephe still had no concept of the job or who these people were, he was content with his Cobb salad and being out of the office. He considered it good practice for his next interviews.

"The job will start as basic reporting for a modest-sized city, with some national and international feeds," Nassir said. "But then some specialized projects are on the horizon. We're going to ask you to keep this quiet, as a courtesy to the four other candidates, but we're very impressed by your résumé and your work at the GLF.

"We'll be flying all candidates in, all expenses paid, in the next week or so. It will help you determine, as well, if the place will be to your liking."

"Thank you for lunch and for the opportunity to meet you. I just have one question: Where are your main offices?"

"Ah. That's the difficult part; our offices are quite remote."

Stephe's heart sank. Max! Well, wherever it was he could commute. Nothing could keep them apart. It would be expensive, that's all. He pictured Anchorage or Fairbanks.

After the interview, down on California Street, as Stephe shook Nassir's hand, Stephe asked again just how remote the job was. Heart in chest; worried about getting to Max.

"I'm afraid they're in an office on Clavius Street. Second Sector. On the Moon."

Back out on the street Stephe wandered aimlessly, so lost in thought he kept bumping into people on the sidewalk as he made his way down Powell to the Muni station, cable cars clanging as they went by.

The Moon? It was like a sick joke. He looked at the business card Nassir had given him like it was a plaything, something from a novelty shop.

The Lunar News Network.

If it was true, what an opportunity! Talk about a departure from his time in the trenches at the GLF!

He sat on a bench in Hallidie Plaza and looked up the Lunar News Network. Of course he'd heard of the LNN. A tiny news organization based on the Moon. They reported Lunar news—for there *were* news stories on the Moon, however trifling they may seem to the people of Earth. A lot of reporting done on Earth for the people of the Moon came from normal Earth news services.

But what about Max? He'd have to leave him; the only good thing that had ever happened to him in his life was Max. He was torn in two, not sure if he should leap for joy or sit down and cry.

He went home. He did his best thinking there. Maybe Max could get a job on the Moon, too? That was no easy feat.

He got out his screen and wrote the pros and cons until he was blue in the face.

Max texted him: "How was the interview?"

"It went well. I think they liked me."

"Excellent! Let's go out to dinner. I'm buying!"

"Thanks! Where do you want to go?" Stephe asked.

"You pick," Max generously offered.

Stephe decided on dinner at Catch in the Castro. They met at Castro and Market Streets, Max emerging from the subway. Stephe's face was hot. He wasn't going to tell Max the whole story. Not yet. They kissed on the sidewalk.

Max started out by talking about his day at work in the State Department of California, but lately he'd been getting gigs for interior design, evenings and weekends, and that was his passion tonight. He was picking up some rather exclusive clients and gushing about them.

"So they wanted everything to look like 2005; bleached wood, arched lines, chintz stripes and Second Empire furnishings. I told them I could do it, but that it's a little too soon as a retro look.

"So anyway," Max concluded, "that's it for me. Tell me about the interview."

"Well," Stephe began, "it looks like a complete departure from what I was doing at the Gay Liberation Front. These people are rich and laid back and pay really well. It's a totally different vibe. I wonder if it might not be a little boring."

"Maybe boring is good, after the hell you've been through. Any downsides that you can think of?"

"Yeah. Big downside. My new job, if I get it, might not be in the Bay Area."

"Shit."

"I know," Stephe agreed. "It's got me torn up."

"Where exactly is it? Wherever it is we can commute," Max suggested.

"They wouldn't say," Stephe lied. He hated to lie to Max.

"Oh."

A cool pall covered the table. Stephe's stomach was in knots; he could barely enjoy his rockfish and risotto. He drank heavily of the crisp white wine.

Finally, that night in bed, Stephe broke the news to Max. "I said they didn't say where the job was, but I was lying."

"I thought you were fibbing," Max replied. "You're not good at it. So how bad are we talking? East Coast?"

Stephe shook his head.

"Moon. It's on the fucking Moon."

"Aww, Jesus," Max moaned.

"I know. Max, I don't know what to do. I can't imagine leaving you! I don't know how often I'd get back to Earth; a ticket's like thirty-six million dollars round trip."

"Well, break it down into small pieces. First things first," Max began. "You should definitely take the interview—you get a free trip to the Moon, and not a lot of people can say that. You said they have four other candidates so your chances are 20 percent. So don't go getting all stressed for something that hasn't even happened yet."

Max was right, and Stephe loved him even more just then for his rational thinking.

"You're right," Stephe said.

"Of course I'm right. I'm always right," Max said. "Now... say you do get the job . . . say you do it for about two years. Would that be long enough to look good on a résumé? We can do two years. It wouldn't be easy, but it's doable. I won't go anywhere."

Stephe considered it. "Two years would be about right."

"Well . . . there. You see?" Max smiled. "So stop worrying about it and enjoy the ride. And walk away from all the pain and suffering at the GLF. Meanwhile, I've got a job you can do right now, and it's *definitely* 100 percent!"

Stephe needed five days off from the GLF to go on his interview. He went into David's office and sat down. "Please don't ask why, but I need a few days off."

"Sure. You've earned it." David said. "Anything going on? You okay?"

"I'm all right, thanks. Just need to get away from here for a couple of days."

"I hear that! I hope you go to Hawaii or something."

"Something like that," Stephe replied.

He met Nona for lunch in North Park, right by her office. He looked at her eye to eye and said, "I have a job interview."

"Congrats! Where is it?"

"Well, that's the hard part. It's for the LNN."

"Get the fuck outta here!" she exclaimed.

"Gospel. I have an interview in Tayin City on May 3rd. They're flying me up."

"Stephe, oh my God! That's incredible!"

"I know, but I don't know what to do about Max."

"Shit."

"Right? But look, maybe I won't get the job," he said. "They have four other candidates. Or maybe I'll just do it for two years and then come home. It won't be forever. Anyway, these are the things I'm telling myself right now. If nothing else, I get a free trip into space."

"Sounds like an amazing opportunity. You get outta this shithole place for one thing."

"But Max!" he moaned.

"I know. He'll wait for you. I can keep an eye on him if you want me to. But what am I going to do without you?"

Chapter 22

Stephe had never known anyone who had been to the Moon.

He was so excited he could hardly sleep. Excited, and sick to his stomach all at once. He was determined to enjoy his trip to the Moon, no matter what the outcome of the interview might be.

He had to be at the Davis Launch Site at ten in the morning to catch his shuttle to Apple Station at eleven; that meant leaving Oakland on the 8:00 a.m. train.

From his house to the Moon.

He said goodbye to Max, tears in his eyes. He hugged him goodbye and walked to Castro Station. He took the Muni Underground to Civic Center, switched to BART for the ride to Oakland, then the High-Speed Rail to the Davis Launch Site. An obscenely huge aircraft with the orbital shuttle nestled to its belly stood waiting for Stephe and the other passengers.

He went through security, his suitcase was scanned, and then he boarded the ship.

He took his assigned seat, 12A—he had a window to himself—and strapped himself in with the seatbelt and shoulder harnesses. He'd seen it done in movies but had never done it in real life; the seats were high-backed and very comfortable in a nice fabric. He waited for everyone else to stow their bags and be seated. Finally the door closed with a WHUMP! and he felt his ears pop as the cabin was pressurized.

"Ladies and gentlemen, welcome aboard Shuttle A253 to Apple Station. Our transit time should be about 22 minutes, barring any unforeseeable orbital traffic. Cabin Crew: prepare for departure."

"Cross-check complete, cabin secure for movement."

The loading bridge moved away and the craft was pushed back from the gate just like an airplane. The Space Plane took off, rolling from zero to 200 mph before lazily nosing up and taking flight. Once they reached an altitude of 80,000 feet, the orbital shuttle unclamped itself; its ion fusion engines took over, and it flew free of the space plane and headed up into orbit. Stephe watched the space plane below and behind roll lazily to the north, free of its cargo, heading back to land in Davis once again. There was a deafening roar and still the acceleration continued for several minutes. Out his window he saw the flat Earth moving away behind him. Within a short time he could make out the curvature of the Earth, the sense that it really is a giant orb banded in layers of air and diminishing quickly. Just as quickly, the sky outside the window faded from azure, to deep blue and then to complete black. Space.

The sounds in the cabin faded just as quickly and soon it became silent. His ears were ringing. The view out his window rotated—so many stars!—and he realized he was completely weightless. He turned to the woman next to him; she was reading a book on her screen, totally ignoring the spectacle.

The seat backs were so high he could see none of the surrounding passengers.

"Ladies and gentlemen, we've now reached Zero-G: Please remain in your seats with harnesses fully buckled until we reach our destination . . . which should be in about six minutes."

Apple Station was built in 2033; a rotating tube with docks inside, essentially a hollow rolling-pin in space. Rotation gave it gravity. The shuttle drove in one end and settled to the deck. A form of pressurized loading bridge came up. There was gravity, as they were now part of the rotating deck; being the innermost ring the gravity was lightest. So debarking from the shuttle Stephe felt a spring in his step as he grabbed his carry-on and went down the broad staircases to Deck Four Promenade: a great hallway running the length of the station with restaurants, shops, and businesses, open to the decks above. It was somewhat reminiscent of the open courtyards of the old-time double-width cruise ships.

Balconies of hotel rooms and offices rose overhead. There was a painted blue sky with clouds.

He saw a Japanese restaurant and went in for sushi.

His ship to the Moon didn't leave for eight hours, so he rented a small windowless hotel room, and went to take a shower and a nap. The bed was comfortable and the sheets felt good on his bare skin. He set his alarm for 22:30 Station Time: Moon launch was at 23:45. Plenty of time. By then he was hungry again and had tapas and wine at a Spanish bar on Deck Four Promenade.

People of all sorts and nationalities mingled freely on Apple Station, unlike on Earth. He saw several affluent Africans and Asians and Russians; all well-dressed and happy.

The *Count Basie 456* was his ship to the Moon, a squat, round vessel with protruding engines out the back. He took an elevator this time to the dock deck where he saw only five other people to share his ride to the Moon. They stepped through the airlock and found the interior of the shuttle much like a small airplane. Deep maroon comfy chairs with harnesses. There were no windows, but a large screen was at his seat. He put his bag in the locker in front of him and strapped himself in.

The announcements were in Russian, translated via his Muon: "Ladies and gentlemen, welcome aboard the *Count Basie 456* with service to Tayin City. Our travel time, as you well know, will be four-hundred and fifty-six minutes. Please keep your harnesses fastened at all times."

Stephe wondered what he was supposed to do if he had to go to the bathroom. He looked behind him and saw a ladder leading down to the back of the ship and was relieved to see Men/Women signs there.

The ship unclamped from the deck and nosed its way into space. Stephe was intent on his screen: he could change views by toggling a switch and set the view to "aft," watching Apple Station, impossibly large, float away.

Acceleration began. He was being pushed back into his recliner, the ship definitely picking up speed. He estimated he weighed about double—it was an effort to raise his arm. This feeling of weightedness continued for nearly three gruesome hours then suddenly abated. He was weightless again as the acceleration stopped. He watched his screen. The stars outside suddenly started moving—the ship was turning around. Traveling stably at 36,000 miles an hour, there was no sensation as the ship simply rotated 180 degrees so the engines were now pointing at the Moon.

"Ladies and gentlemen, we're now at the halfway point. We'll begin a gradual deceleration, so you'll have a few moments to move about the cabin." The engines pulsed—no sound—and Stephe and his fellow passengers were pressed gently into their seats. The seatbelt harness sign turned off and Stephe made a beeline down the ladder to the bottom of the ship to use one of the lavatories. Several people also made to follow him. Because of the gentle deceleration, gravity was more or less normal. The seats were in rows up and down, with the back of the ship forming the floor. He peed and washed his hands and climbed back up into his seat, fighting the gravity to raise his feet up and put them in the footrest above him. He was back to a comfortable recline.

A cabin attendant came out with food packs, climbing the stairs like a vendor at a ball park. Stephe was hungry enough to enjoy his turn; warm ginger chicken over rice, small salad and a Coca-cola.

So he pulled out his little tray table and enjoyed his meal. The attendant collected the meal packs and it was announced that stronger deceleration would begin in twenty minutes; at that time all passengers must be in their seats with harnesses fastened. A few people climbed down the ladder to empty their bladders or to enjoy normal weightedess for a few minutes.

After the promised twenty minutes the seatbelt harness sign came back on and once everyone was crosschecked into their seats the ship began its deceleration in earnest. Three more hours of double-weightedness. It was tiring. Stephe tried to sleep—and did, actually, despite his excitement.

The ship was backing its way down to the lunar surface. Gravity went up as deceleration was stepped up, then became extreme and soon they touched down on the Moon on a landing pad as light as a feather.

"Ladies and gentlemen, welcome to the lunar surface and to Tayin City. Lunar local time is 06:23. Thank you for flying the Four Fifty-Six."

Gravity was light. This was Moon gravity, potentially his new home. He went through another airlock, which quickly became a normal hallway, and proceeded to Customs and Immigration. His Visa was scanned. This time he was pulled in; they went through his bag and asked him some questions about his projected stay and status, and he was quickly released.

He marveled that he'd just walked from his house at 472 Liberty Street to the Moon.

He was met by Nassir Gupta himself outside Customs.

"Welcome to the Moon," Nassir said. "I'll be your liaison while you're here. "We've arranged a hotel room for you. Your interview is tomorrow morning at ten."

They took a travel tube—basically an above-ground pressurized subway. Several stops later, they got out and Stephe got a view of a typical lunar street. It was more like a mall than a street; everything was carpeted, which lent an eerie silence. People passed them by, unhurried, well-dressed. People used Segways on the Moon a lot. They made virtually no noise on the carpets. Stephe couldn't remember the last time he'd seen a Segway, he thought they'd been lost to time.

He was delighted in the diversity of the people going by. Africans and Chinese and Russians and East Indians—it was a true melting pot here on the Moon. And everybody got along. He even saw two gay women walking by, holding hands.

Stephe was having a little problem with the gravity, though. It was so light! It made him dizzy. He had the uncontrollable urge to jump up and down, to see how high he could go.

"Everything here is made with Moon rock processed into concrete. So building is quite inexpensive, and there's plenty of room. The hardest part is importing enough oxygen and water to support the inhabitants. There is actually water on the Moon; we're working to distill as much of it as we can."

They were walking down the street past a few restaurants, bars and offices. In the ceilings above the street were giant windows looking out to a pitch-black sky. They reached the hotel and Stephe Muoned in; the room was paid for by the LNN.

"You'll find a fully-stocked minibar in your room, all expenses paid," the man at the desk said. "We have a restaurant, gym and swimming pool at your disposal."

Nassir took his leave: "Here's the address for the office. You take the travel tube three stops and get off at Clavius. The offices are right across the street, you can't miss them. Interview's at 10:00 a.m. tomorrow, so you have a day to rest and get acclimated."

"Thank you very much, Mr. Gupta." Stephe reached out to shake his hand.

"Please, call me Nassir."

Stephe almost chuckled. It sounded like "Please call me Sir."

"Thank you, Nassir. Will I see you tomorrow?"

"I'll be there. See you at ten."

And Nassir turned and walked out of the hotel and back toward the travel tube.

Stephe's room was on the third floor; he took a small elevator and was pleased at the room—except for the fact that it didn't have a window. There was a huge screen on one wall, though, showing a crisp field of grass rippling in a breeze under a sunny blue sky. The room was spacious and luxurious, and, most importantly, had very high ceilings. He set down his ultra-light suitcase and began jumping.

He took a shower. Signs were posted about water being precious on the Moon, and requested that guests not use too much. The water was different, being so light in the lower gravity. It splashed a lot farther and felt strange on his skin. Then he climbed into bed and took a nap.

Waking up confused, he wasn't sure where he was at first. It was 13:30.

The Moon!

He was excited. Feeling very lonely, and missing Max, he opened his Growlr app, once again hoping for someone to chat to. There weren't a lot of men on there, not so many as he'd figured. But a guy named Lunar Mojo began talking to him. He didn't feel interested at first, but Lunar Mojo finally started chatting with Stephe and wearing him down. He was kinda Stephe's type; they unlocked their pictures and interest grew.

"What are you into?" Stephe asked; the usual questions when chatting up a stranger.

"You want to come over? It's Saturday, so I'm not working."

"I'm new here, just arrived this morning," Stephe replied.

"Where you staying?" Mojo asked.

"At the Hilton in Third Sector."

"Ah. I'm in Fourth Sector. It's real easy. Wanna come over?"

"Sure," Stephe answered.

Stephe wasn't sure, actually. His heart was aching for Max but he was also mad and horned up. He needed to clear his head.

After getting dressed, he left the hotel and, following Lunar Mojo's instructions, took the travel tube further out from the heart of the city and alit in Fourth Sector. The street looked much the same as his own; the place had been built quickly and not with a lot of variation in the designs. The carpets were different but the windows up above were the same. He saw Earth, three-quarters waning, in the windows and stopped and stared for a few moments. People bumped into him, hurrying about their business.

Suddenly he felt sick about what he was considering doing. Max was up there on that blue ball, that festering shithole called Earth.

Stephe almost turned around and headed back to the Hilton, but thought better of it. He was going to have to move on. He went to the designated apartment building and rang the buzzer.

"Hullo?" came the voice through a speaker.

"It's Stephe," he answered.

"Apartment 5A." The door buzzed and Stephe went in. The elevator softly carried him up to the fifth floor. The lobby was decorated in Victorian rugs and elegant side tables and striped wallpaper. Very 2005.

Stephe knocked. The door slid aside.

Lunar Mojo stood there in a jockstrap looking Stephe over. They shook hands. He was of medium build, very hairy—Stephe liked that—black hair, black body hair and a lovely chest. None of the grey of Max, none of the extra padding Stephe loved so much.

"My name's Jeff. C'mon in."

Stephe was relieved, at least, that he wasn't being sent away, but part of him had hoped he would be. You never know until you meet someone in the flesh if it's going to be a match. Plenty of times someone looks good on a Muon but not so much in real life.

Lunar Mojo/Jeff invited him to have a beer. Stephe was grateful to accept.

Jeff's apartment was on the top floor and had huge windows overlooking the lunar surface. Stephe was mesmerized.

"Do you mind if I just look out the windows for a sec?" Stephe asked.

"Not at all! It's why I took the place, even though it was way out of my price range."

Immediately below the windows was the street, covered, its own windows looking small from the fifth floor. A tumble of small buildings, all connected, strung out on either side of the street. After those buildings petered out, though, was actual lunar surface. Grey rock. It went on for dozens of miles. He gazed out over the spectacle; Tayin City was in a crater surrounded by stygian mountains in the distance, a tumble of light and shadow. The sun was up and to the right, a cold orb of white light.

Jeff came up beside him and but his arm around Stephe. He was about the same height. Stephe turned and they kissed and Stephe couldn't help but remember his first kiss, with Al, back in 2025 in front of Starbucks. No piercing this time.

The kiss was good, but Stephe could tell Jeff wasn't "the one." He felt fine, but he wasn't a zinger like Max was.

Max. Stephe buried the thought.

"Why don't we go sit on the sofa," Jeff suggested. They did. "I'm in data services for one of the larger mining corporations," Jeff said. "Had to learn Chinese. What do you do?"

"I'm a writer/reporter, for the Gay Liberation Front in San Francisco. It gets heinous."

"Hey. I thought I recognized you. Wicked," Jeff said, kissing him again.

"I'm here for a job interview tomorrow."

They began making out in earnest then, conversation forgotten. Stephe was pleased that he could respond. He took his shirt off and Jeff chewed on his nipples, which, after so many years with Max, had become quite responsive.

"Let's go into the bedroom," Jeff said and led the way.

All blue. Subdued, futuristic light panels. A nice big bed. Jeff sat on the bed and Stephe joined him.

Because gravity was light, it was an entirely different experience for Stephe. There was just so much more you could do. Jeff laid on him with his full weight, which was only about fifty pounds in the gravity. Stephe giggled.

"What's so funny?" Jeff asked.

"Nothing. It's just that this is my first time on the Moon. Your weight is so light!" Stephe picked up Jeff and lightly set him on the bed.

They wrestled around, trying various positions.

"I could do this all day," Jeff said.

"Me too!"

So they did.

Afterwards Jeff offered to get Stephe a towel. They took turns wiping themselves clean and kissed once again.

"I hope you get that job!" Jeff said. "That way we could do this more." He smiled.

"I hope I do too. This was good."

They went back out to the living room and Stephe got dressed. Jeff walked him to the door. They Muoned each other their email addresses, and Jeff kissed Stephe goodbye and Stephe left.

Back down at street level he decided to walk back to Third Sector. It was a straight shot along the path of the travel tube.

He felt much less lonely; Jeff could be a good friend if Stephe got the job.

He passed restaurants and office buildings but mostly apartments. He came upon a huge grocery store that could have passed for one on Earth.

He got back to the Hilton by 4 p.m. It seemed too early for dinner, but he was hungry. He decided to walk more. Toward the center of town. Several travel tube lines converged at Armstrong Park. Here were many domed sections of the city, places that felt more like a regular town than a shopping mall. There were even several high-rise buildings. He found an Indian restaurant and had lamb korma, matta paneer, garlic naan and red wine; he wondered how far the ingredients had traveled to be there on his plate, but it was all surprisingly fresh and good.

The next morning he got to Lunar News Network head offices fifteen minutes early. He was escorted into a very nice office, through a newsroom that didn't have the buzz of a normal newsroom. It was relaxed, genteel, sedate—apparently not a lot happened on the Moon. The Earth media center was more what he was used to, a hubbub of concern. More tragedies were unfolding in the United States.

The interview went well. He was interviewed by Nassir and a man named Cheong-il Park, Editor in Chief. They seemed to know a lot about Stephe's work.

"We need someone with credentials and who's known on Earth," began Park. "There are going to be a few vitally important news stories coming up, and we want someone who's trusted, well-known and poised. We think that person is you."

"Well, thank you!" Stephe replied. "I'd love to be considered. What sort of news stories are coming up, if you don't mind my asking?"

"Unfortunately, we have to keep that under wraps for the time being. But it's fairly important news. We want a trusted face."

"Well, I'm your man."

"Tell us of your time at the Gay Liberation Front."

Stephe ran through his CV and recounted some of his trips to the Heartland. But they already knew his stories; that's why he was there.

Stephe asked them general questions about workload, pay and expectations in the position.

Nassir replied, "Our workload isn't a fraction of what you're used to, until our big story breaks. Then you're likely to be pretty busy."

"I have a partner at home; so the distance is going to be very difficult for us."

"We'll need you on Earth a lot, so that shouldn't be a problem."

Wow. That was good! Stephe wasn't going to be trapped on the Moon for two solid years. He and Max would be able to see each other.

The interview concluded. Cheong-il Park shook Stephe's hand and thanked him for his time.

"We're very pleased," Park said. "Your chances are good. We'll be in touch in a few days."

Stephe thanked them for their time and consideration, and for the trip to the Moon. He felt good about his performance in the interview, and was intrigued about the job, despite how vague they were about certain things, like the "vitally important news stories coming up." That was the only part that left him ill at ease.

With the interview concluded, it was time to go home and see Max.

Before going back to his hotel he walked the perimeter of Armstrong Park. It might be his only chance to see it, if he didn't get the job. He marveled at the huge transparent dome. It was immense; flawless. Plant life thrived in the lower gravity. He saw the horses, cantering around in low-G. He walked around the lake, enjoying the ducks. People were out enjoying the day; the sun was cold and small so lights everywhere enhanced the normalcy of the park. The temperature was a steady 74 degrees.

Then he did go back to his hotel for his bag and headed for home: travel tube to the space port. His ship, the *Billie Holiday 456*, was to leave at 14:45. This time he knew what to expect as he climbed into his seat aboard the ship and stowed his bag. Three grueling hours of the supergravity of thrust once more, as tiring as ever; the mid-way point of normal gravity and lunch; double-weightedness again as the ship slowly decelerated to dock with Apple Station.

He didn't have to wait long for his shuttle to Earth, only about two hours.

He got settled into his seat on the shuttle and they lifted off, out the donut hole and into space. The ion shuttle became essentially a great glider, swooping down into Earth's atmosphere and landing in Davis, California, twenty-five minutes later.

Max was waiting for him outside Customs in Davis; he'd ridden out from meetings in Sacramento and they kissed. "How was it?" he asked Stephe.

"Good, thanks! They say I'll get plenty of time on Earth, which is a *huge* bonus! We can stay together a lot more than I'd thought."

"Thank God!"

"I don't want to go away from you, but a job like this . . . "

"I know. But I don't want to stand in your way."

"Sometimes I wish you would."

They kissed again, walking back to the rail station.

"I'm done in Sacramento for a while. Let's ride back together."

They sat next to each other on the highspeed train as it raced at 250 mph through the Central Valley on its way to the Bay Area. Stephe told him everything he saw and did—omitting his time with Jeff.

Stephe was hired by the Lunar News Network. He was to start on June 1st—three weeks away.

Suddenly it felt like a death sentence to him. Max! They made love three times that night.

He still had to resign from the Gay Liberation Front. He took David into his office and gave his two-week notice. David was gobsmacked.

"Damn!" he said. "The Moon, huh? Well, hell." He stuck out his hand. "Congratulations! You deserve this."

They gave Stephe a grand send-off with a huge party; everyone cried. Nicole cried the hardest—"Do you know how great my tits would look in low-g?"

Max was to retain the use of 472 Liberty Street. Stephe hated the idea of Max dating other people, especially in his own bed, but that was to be the way of it. If they survived the projected two years then they knew they were for real. If not, then . . . he wouldn't think about that.

A tearful, sickening goodbye. Max didn't want to accompany Stephe to Davis. He'd gotten pretty sullen as their time drew to a close. It was heartrending.

On May 30, 2037, Stephe flew to the Moon just like any boring businessman. He was too heartsick to enjoy it. Off in the Orbital Launcher, four hours on Apple Station, then up to the Moon on the *Benny Goodman 456*.

The LNN, as part of their arrangement, set him up in a nice apartment in Fourth Sector—not too far from Jeff's place. It was a small unit, not nearly as nice as Jeff's, but it did have a single window looking out over the city. He didn't bring many items from Earth; although given a generous weight allowance, there just wasn't anything he wanted to bring unless he could have smuggled Max. He just brought clothes, a few nicknacks, and a dirty pair of Max's underwear.

He called Max when he got there. Max looked strained.

"How was the flight?"

"Fine. It's a little boring when the excitement wears off. The extreme acceleration and deceleration really wear you down."

"I've heard that. Still, I'd love to experience it!"

"You will. Somehow we'll get you up here."

They talked more, about nothing, and finally hung up. The phone call cost $3,800.00.

So this is what it feels like, Stephe mused glumly. Haggard phone calls and missing Max and unstated anger at the unfairness of it all.

His first day at work alarmed him; it was too easy. Nothing much happened on the Moon. One of the mining companies was accused of racketeering and mining on another firm's turf; a few reports of domestic violence and a thievery took place at a jewelry shop on Ganymede Street. Meanwhile he kept his eyes on the Earth newsfeeds, regularly checked in with the GLF's webpage to keep his hand in; another gay massacre, this time in Texas.

Most of the news staff were Chinese, Indian, and Russian; the news was translated into those languages to accommodate all the residents of a very diverse Moon.

Stephe got to know the people he worked with and they were all very gracious, good individuals.

But he was starting to feel like this was a big mistake. Six million dollars a year be damned; by about two weeks in he wanted to go home.

Then it happened. It all fell into place.

Chapter 23

Cheong-il Park called him into his office. Nassir was there.

"You've been here for two weeks and we're very pleased with your performance. Therefore, it's time for you to up the ante a little bit," said Nassir. He paused. "You're in for quite a shock," he cautioned.

In walked a man in a 1940s-looking suit with blue-hued skin. Stephe assumed it was an anime cosplay gone wrong.

"This is Ch'Shock Ungh. Ch'Shock, I'd like you to meet Stephen Stafford."

Stephe stood and they shook hands. Ch'Shock's skin was remarkably different to the touch. Cool and dry, with an unusual texture.

"Very pleased to meet you, Mr. Stafford." The man had a strange accent, unlike anything Stephe had ever heard.

"Thank you . . . umm . . . sir. It's a pleasure to meet you."

"Why don't we all sit down?" Cheong-il Park suggested.

They sat, Stephe totally in the dark as to where this was all going.

"Ch'Shock isn't from here," Cheong-il Park said matter of factly. "He is a Guelph." Stephe heard "Elf." "He's from a planet orbiting the star we call Arcturus."

Huh. So these people're all nuts, Stephe thought.

"This is why you're here," said Nassir. "Only the LNN has access to the scoop of the millennium, and you're here to cover it for us."

"Stephe," Nassir continued, "humans aren't the only sentient beings in space. As people have always suspected, we're not alone in the universe. Mr. Ch'Shock represents something called the 'Grand Society.' The Grand Society, to use an old science fiction phrase, is like a federation of planets. Peaceful, democratic and very, very learned."

Stephe still wasn't sure he was buying any of this.

"This is why you're here," Nassir said again. "To introduce them to Earth. The time has come to consider First Contact. It would be the most important turning point in human history and it might happen next month. If we can convince them we're worth it."

"Yes," said Ch'Shock. "We're inclined to include Earth in the Grand Society. There are thirty-six member species. Humans would be number thirty-seven. We've been here since your year 1982, gathering information, studying your history and politics. Your planet is at a tipping point with global warming, which is a normal thing to happen at this stage in your development. We think we can help. But some members aren't convinced Earth is a good fit for us."

Stephe was dizzy. He wanted to believe what he was seeing and hearing. But he wasn't sure he really did. It was all a little too . . . precious.

"How can I help?" Stephe asked.

Ch'Shock spoke:

"Several member species are reviewing your work at the Gay Liberation Front. To some, it's confirmation that your planet should be avoided at all costs; to others it's a cry for help.

"You see, war, poverty, race riots and food shortages could become a thing of the past on Earth. It happens this way every time: Once a planet knows they are but one tiny cog in a much larger wheel, things begin to change, and change quickly. You'd all have access to free energy, technology, healthcare beyond your wildest dreams—and jobs; jobs you can't even imagine right now.

"You'll have to give up some water and mining rights to your outer planets. Birthrates will have to be curtailed, because humans will now easily live up to two hundred years. So you can't keep reproducing like you have been."

Stephe wondered how that would go down with the religious right. As if to answer, Ch'Shock continued. "I'm afraid God, Allah and Buddha are about to take a back seat. We have our own gods we pray to, too. So, you'd begin at what we call Level Four—that's the introductory level for new species but by the time trade negotiations are done and our people are known on Earth you'll have some years to get your act together."

Ch'shock was smiling, no malice in his words: "It always happens this way."

"And this happens next month?" Stephe asked.

"If approved." Nassir replied. "On July 1, 2037, a delegation from the Moon will land at the UN in New York and all will be made clear. I'm told it usually causes quite an upset."

Ch'shock explained, "Some species don't respond well. But it's been estimated that you humans are at the right stage for First Contact. Your planet is shattered and limping; there's nowhere to go but up!" He made a happy upward gesture with his blue arm; again there was no evil or shame in what he was saying. It was just sort of matter-of-fact.

"Stephe," Nassir went on to say, "No one on Earth knows about this. No one at CNN, RT, RTL, CBC—no one has this. This is an exclusive to the Lunar News Network and it's vitally important that it *stays* that way. Not only is it about ratings, but, done improperly, First Contact could have damaging consequences."

Following a brief pause, Nassir continued with instructions: "We have a homework assignment for you. We'd like for you to do a report on First Contact. Your audience will be the members of the Grand Society. Sort of a commercial. A PR piece, about ten minutes long. What First Contact would mean for us. What life is like on Earth right now. It would be like so many of your reports, only this is sort of an advertisement piece about the people of Earth. You have all of our equipment at your disposal. Do you think you can do that?"

"Of course. That's what I do best." Stephe hoped he wasn't exaggerating. It had been his job for seven years; he hoped he could do it justice.

Nassir did something on his screen, and three additional individuals came into Cheong-il Park's spacious office.

One was covered in soft hair with a brown sheen, wearing a sarong with a golden emblem on its forehead; one seemed human but much taller, with willowy appendages, wearing a suit; the third was a yellowish humanoid with very angular features.

They came in and were introduced to Stephe: the brown-haired being was a female Zzzzt named La'Ush; the tall one was a Carlash named Dank; and the third, an Ebb called Yousch.

"All these beings are here, with the exception of Dank," Nassir continued, "because their induction into the Grand Society has been very recent. Within their lifetimes. They are living witnesses to the effects of Integration. They know what it's like to be the new kids on the block. Their memories of their 'before times' are still fresh, and they'd be invaluable if Earth makes its First Contact."

"It's a pleasure to meet you," La'Ush said as Stephe extended his hand. She took it in greeting, the soft fur and long fingers feeling pleasantly warm to Stephe's touch. La'Ush's English had a strange vibratory sound when she spoke to Stephe. He shook each being's hand in turn.

"Your Muon has already been beamed with all the information. You're now free to read up on the Grand Society and its members. Whatever you'd like," said Nassir, "including all the languages."

"We were contacted by Ch'Shock six months ago," Cheong-il Park said. "I can assure you I was as skeptical as you must be feeling right now, Stephe. No one can guarantee how this will go, but if this First Contact does what we think it'll do, the persecution of gays and lesbians in your country will come to an end quickly. There won't be any need for it. I know how important that is to you."

Stephe nearly fainted with relief. Could it be true?

"Stephe?" Nassir asked. "How do you feel?"

"I'm overwhelmed. What I feel is, I'd like is to go home and get started on my piece," answered Stephe. "Plus, I think I might need a nap," he continued, with what sounded unfortunately like a small whimper.

"Understood!" said Nassir cheerfully. "I had exactly the same reaction. Why don't you come back about 20:00 tonight. We'll meet here and have dinner. We have a few other surprises for you as well."

More surprises? Stephe couldn't imagine being any more surprised than he already was. His mind reeled at having to not only memorize new names and faces, but new species as well. He said goodbye to La'Ush, Ch'shock, Dank, Yousch, Nassir and Cheong-il Park, proud that he remembered all the names correctly, and he made his way to the street below. He took a transport tube, zipped along the lunar surface to his apartment block, and headed straight for bed, his head buzzing.

He Muoned up the Grand Society, the information now at his disposal. This was the year 3864. The original species who met and began the Grand Society were the Guelph and the Carlash, 3,863 Interplanetary Years ago. He looked up what the Guelph and Carlash were like. "Homeworld" was the Guelph planet in the solar system of the star we called Arcturus. It was the center of the Grand Society, the center of government. Of course there had been clashes: The Carlash wanted Homeworld to be their planet, but it was twelve degrees too cold and most of its plants and food were poisonous to everybody else.

Instead of napping Stephe got straight to work on his report. It was a proposal, a cry for help. He had to sell Earth and all its problems, and yet it was part travelogue. It was a ten-minute commercial on the people of Earth for all the citizens and leaders of the Grand Society. It had to count for something; it would be seen by 46 billion people.

He Muoned up video after video, image after image, and soon had a working montage. He sat typing on his screen until his head was spinning, but he was off to a good start. Later at the office he'd begin his report in earnest. He just had enough time to take a low-water shower and dress for dinner.

Chapter 24

He went back to the office for dinner, no clearer in the head than he'd been before. It all still sounded too precious. Too impossible. He wanted to believe, but was this real?

A table was set in a huge executive dining room behind Mr. Park's office that Stephe had never even known was there. It was lavish and formal. Many places were set and many people milling around with various sorts of drinks in their hands—or appendages. The five species were represented, plus two more: an orange creature on wheels and a feline humanoid in a frock.

Stephe went to the bar to command a scotch when he got another shock. A tap on his shoulder, he turned around and Max was standing there, smiling simply.

"Hey."

"Oh, my God! Jesus! What are you doing here?"

"I got here about two hours ago. The LNN flew me up!"

They fell to each other in an embrace, hugging kissing, smelling each other, and applause broke out around them.

Stephe was happier than he'd ever been in his life.

He thought of 472 Liberty Street, and Margery, and Jack now living in Oakland—nothing of his old life remained any longer—and here was Max! As long as they could be together . . . everything was suddenly possible. They could have a future once again. If things went as predicted, if Earth would shake itself from its malaise and join the Grand Society.

Everyone gathered for a traditional formal Guelph dinner in the dining room. Stephe thought of Thanksgiving two years ago and was thrown by how different it all was. Max sat by his side.

They were served a stunning array of strange food. Meats and starches and a cold soup, and all of it on polished silver and fine Earth china.

Max was obviously in on the alien surprise. He seemed to be interacting more casually than Stephe was. Max always was a class act.

To Max's right was the feline character from the planet Benog; Stephe listened to their conversation. "Our planet has been in the Grand Society for only seventy-five years," she was saying. "We were much as Earth is now; warring, dwindling resources, climate change. The first delegations from the Grand Society were met with derision and scorn—several were shot on sight. It takes a while for the new reality to take hold. But once it did, things changed rapidly. Free water and energy—the only things remaining to fight over are God and land, and the very perspectives on those change quickly in the Grand Society."

Stephe, not wishing to be rude, pulled himself from Max's conversation with the Benog and addressed the creature to his left—the orange being on wheels. A Virynt.

His name was Ralch. His planet had been in the Grand Society for just a few years. His planet, as he described via his Muon, was ocean-going, which is why they needed wheels to get around on other worlds. His home world was ravaged by a totalitarian government; its hold on the people was absolute. Ralch explained to Stephe, "I'm told a suitable example for an Earth human would be an amalgam of your Nazi Germany and *1984*, although I don't know those things with any degree of accuracy. We were all drones, in thrall to serve the government; individuality was wiped out. We had achieved great art and literature—we're told—in our past, more enlightened days. But it was all destroyed to serve the State. Our oceans were increasingly polluted and we were on the brink of extinction. Your average Virynt didn't even have any idea; we were just blindly obedient to the propaganda of the State. Since our melding with the Grand Society, we've become liberated. Our iron government denied the very existence of the Grand Society for over a hundred years. It wasn't until things fell apart that they finally allowed them to help."

After dinner Stephe met with Nassir.

"How you holding up?" he asked.

"My brain is withering," Stephe said.

"It's perfectly natural," Nassir assured him. "It took me two weeks to realize it wasn't just some kind of a put-on job. In India we don't have Santa Claus. But that's exactly what this is like. It's Christmas Eve for Earth."

Stephe couldn't believe how torn he was between getting Max back to the apartment and meeting the rest of these strange beings. But he'd had enough for one day. Nassir assured him he'd have the chance to interview all of them in the following days.

"Oh. By the way," Nassir said as an aside. "It was our pleasure to bring your Max up here; we'll set about getting you a larger apartment. He's a big man." He smiled.

It was time to take Max home.

Max's suitcases were in Nassir's office, fresh off the *ZZ Top 456* that afternoon. They took the travel tube to Stephe's—*their* apartment.

"This gravity is weird," Max said jumping up and down. He zoomed across the small room and smacked his hands against the wall. "I'm glad we're gonna get a bigger place."

They stood and looked out the lone window, toward the city. The ridges of the far side of the crater were in shadow, but you could still make them out because of the dazzling array of stars coming to an end.

"I'm so glad you're here!" Stephe said. "How did the flight up strike you?"

"You're right, it's damn uncomfortable, once the excitement wears off, 456 minutes takes a long time to happen."

They smooched and made out and made love. Max was even more of a tiger in low-g; Stephe could do all kinds of fun stuff, but missed the full weight of Max.

"Hey," said Max, "do you think people get real fat on the Moon?"

Stephe fell asleep to the sounds of Max's C-PAP.

Their new apartment had a series of windows, crater view. They'd spend hours looking out at the lunar surface. It was much bigger than Stephe's original apartment; brighter and with spigots and controls designed for a broader range of hand shapes.

He worked hard on his presentation. It was done by the next day; Nassir suggested a few edits which were hastily corrected by Stephe.

Nassir beamed Stephe's infomercial on Earth to the Council for their consideration.

Stephe spent the rest of his time studying hard. He had 3864 years of history to catch up on. He was hungry for the information but it made his head buzz. They'd had their wars and skirmishes, but, as a rule, when a new planet was scheduled for First Contact, that planet would mend their ways—and pretty damn quick.

A giant weight began to lift for Stephe. If what all these species were saying was true, then all the gay men and women in prison could be liberated after First Contact. If it were true!

He had been carrying despair and guilt within himself for years, so helpless to fix a world gone mad. Well, now he had his chance. He was going to help deliver news to the people of Earth that it didn't have to be this way . . . that there was a better way.

As promised, Stephe was able to interview all the members present. As varied as they were, their stories were remarkably similar to each other. Dying worlds; Grand Society; a quick mending of society's ills.

The Zzzzt jointed the Grand Society twenty-five years ago. Stephe interviewed La'Ush.

"My people were in a civil war. Half the planet was fighting the other side; it raged for a hundred years. We'd become fairly advanced, technologically. But it all went toward weapons and warfare. And through it all was the backdrop of global warming and pollution. Overcrowding was never a problem; we were too busy killing each other."

"What was the Civil War about?" Stephe asked.

"You know, I don't even know! The war had raged a hundred years before I was born. I just knew we hated the other side and they hated us and it was war, war, war! All of our industry was devoted to it. Fiendish weapons, biological attacks, nuclear bombs. The death toll kept rising with no end in sight.'Then we were visited; the Guelph took one side, the Carlash took our side. I'll never forget that day of First

Contact," La'Ush continued. "I was in university when the news came in. Everyone assumed it was a plot, a mistake... a ruse. But the leaders of both sides agreed to a meeting on the Guelph ship—it was the first time we'd had any contact with the other side in over a century. I'm told they didn't even know how to act! A ceasefire was called in two weeks. Nobody wanted to fight anymore. It was like an 'ah-hah moment.' What were we doing? Why were we doing it? At any rate, that's what I remember thinking at the time."

Despite all the news and overload, Stephe still had his regular job to do. It was quite difficult reporting on currencies and mining efforts while the biggest story in human history banged away inside his head. He did a live feed from Armstrong Park about the lunar currency and another about a fire that took place inside a Russian restaurant in the Russian sector—quickly put out, as everything was made of stone. Still, it was news, and he was a reporter.

Cheong-il Park and Ch'Shock had another surprise for Max and Stephe.

"You've been invited to Homeworld, the center of the Grand Society," Park said. "You leave first thing tomorrow. It's just for about twelve days—eight of them will be spent in space. We want footage of you at the Imperial Senate and the Acropolis as part of the Great Reveal. We could splice you in, but we want it to be the real deal. We still have over twenty-one days before First Contact. You'll be back in plenty of time. And don't worry about the newsroom while you're gone, we can handle the domestic squabbles and petty larcenies while you're gone.

Park added, "It has the added bonus of keeping you both quiet. We're working hard to keep this all a secret until July 1st."

The Guelph Ship was parked in an underground hangar and was a work of art. Maroon in color, with gold trim, it was a slender shard, narrow at the front and jagged at the back. But not in a messy mechanical way—it was somehow made to look beautiful.

"The propulsion system wouldn't make sense to you," Ch'Shock told them. "Not to sound patronizing, but we can't share everything with you all at once. It's too complex. Travel time to Guelph will be four of your days, and four days back. That gives you four days in Khorlu, the Capital City of the Galaxy. I grew up there; I think you'll like it."

Stephe pictured Ch'Shock as a little blue child. In a 1940's suit.

The Guelph ship seemed more like a yacht than a spacefaring vessel. Spacious cabins, grand salons, a spa for various species. A huge dining room. It could accommodate thirty people comfortably, but it was just Ch'Shock, Stephe and Max, so it seemed to be a huge, echoing place.

Stephe and Max were thrilled to be allowed into the cockpit for takeoff. As with the rest of the ship, the control center was more like a work of art than a series of controls.

"Most things are done automatically; a bridge crew consists of only four people," Ch'Shock was explaining. "Navigation is done here"—a station with a 3-D holographic area of stars with the ship's course plotted through.

"Here is the actual helm," he said as he pointed out the reclining seat surrounded by controls—all brilliant colors and 3-D interface. "Climate, gravity, engineering are all automatically controlled."

"How fast will we be traveling?" Max asked.

"Twelve times the speed of light, or . . . " Ch'Shock fiddled with one of the controls and read the answer aloud, "8,047,399,548 miles per hour. Of course, once we surpass the speed of light, the mechanics are quite different. Don't worry, you won't feel a thing."

The hangar doors opened, the ship lifted up and with no sensation, floated free of the docking bay. As they stood there together on the bridge, the ship tilted up and began accelerating, the Moon and Earth beyond dropped away in a rearview holographic projection and no awareness was felt. They stood undisturbed, no sensation to it. No noise. Soon the Earth and Moon were lost in a sea of stars.

"Now we'll exceed light speed," Ch'Shock said. The controls switched to blue, and still without the slightest sensation, the view out the front became a blur of stars.

"I'm afraid that's it. Not very exciting after all. We're actually in something called sub-space. The very material of the ship and we ourselves are existing in a completely different form. It's all held together by this system here," and he pointed to another control station. "This keeps us from becoming liquified and smashed into goo."

"Has one of those ever gone out?" Max asked.

"In the very early days. Wasn't pretty. No, nowadays it's as safe as a simple battery. While I'm sure this was fascinating," Ch'Shock said lightly, "I think it's time for lunch. It will take us four days to get to Khorlu and there won't be anything else to see, really."

Lunch sounded like a good idea. They went to the main dining room and were served Zzzzt food, which Stephe learned he quite liked. It was gooey and delicious—somewhat like Thai food.

The four days were actually rather monotonous; Stephe was glad for all the reading material at his disposal—Max read it too—and they studied diligently. They'd stay up nights talking about all the new information. The history and culture were simply too much to grasp.

Guelph written history went back ten thousand years. They were an artistic and industrious species, having had their iron age and dark ages and renaissance; finally their industrial era kicked in and, like most species, pollution and climate change threatened their planet, too. They took to space—Guelph had no moon, so they had to set their sights much higher. They traveled to other planets in their solar system, twelve in all, and set up mining and water reclamation—both of which forestalled their crisis, but ultimately weren't enough. They developed faster-than-light travel and soon met the Carlash.

The Carlash were very similar. They'd had faster-than-light travel for a few years before the Guelph and had visited other planets, only to find pre-industrialized civilizations. They tried revealing themselves to one of these civilizations, but it didn't go well—they found themselves attacked with bows and arrows, and no common basis of communication could be found. So discovering the Guelph was a great fortune; two neighboring stars and two species that got along well.

They formed what they called The Grand Society and, as other species developed space travel, they welcomed them into the fold. Some dated back two millennia; others—such as the Virynt—as recently as a few years ago.

The Grand Society learned and documented everything. The Central Library in Khorlu was the repository of all knowledge—scores of species and planets throughout the quadrant—with several back-ups kept on various other worlds. They kept tabs on underdeveloped species while keeping themselves hidden. Earth was one such underdeveloped world.

Stephe read ahead to learn of the city of Khorlu. It was the Capital City of the Galaxy.

As such, of course, it was stunningly beautiful. Laid out in concentric circles with canals, radiating boulevards and the Chongji district: The seat of all Government. As epic and grand and pretentious as you'd expect. All the radial streets led to Chongji, and at the very center, was the Senate Chamber.

After four days Ch'Shock, Max and Stephe were once again on the bridge of the ship as it slowed and entered the heavy traffic patterns of Homeworld. The amount of traffic was dizzying. They zoomed through the clouds and found themselves on a freeway of ships and travel craft of all sorts. Finally they reached their destination. Their ship landed on the roof of a hotel tower; Stephe guessed it was at least 150 stories tall and was only one of many, far taller buildings. One tower off to the side must have been half a mile in height. It was stunning.

Disembarking, they were met by several well-dressed Guelph and a few Carlash, and were welcomed to Khorlu and to the JingBa Hotel. They checked into their lavish suite on the 148th floor. They were given maps and told that their Muons would work everywhere, translating the language, and interfacing with the local currency units. They had carte blanche to go where they wished.

Stephe and Max obviously wanted to see the Senate, the library and the various lower chambers of government. That's where they headed first. They got a VIP tour of the government buildings. It took all day. The Senate Building was a domed edifice, at the very center of Khorlu. From the rooftop parapet you could see all the boulevards radiating out, like from the Arc de Triomphe in Paris. It was dizzyingly beautiful.

The skies overhead were a bluish-purple, and they saw the sun set from atop the Senate Building and were awash in hues of gold and orange.

Most of the rest of the time they roamed the city together, Stephe and Max, marveling at all they saw. Khorlu was immense, population thirty-two million, but it was never cramped, never seedy. Stephe figured the seediness was kept outside Khorlu, and wondered what he'd find in the suburbs and small towns.

The Guelph loved to shop. They seemed to enjoy looking at themselves; mirrors were everywhere. Stephe suspected they were rather vain. There was no such thing as an ugly Guelph, or, if there were, they kept them hidden in shame. Everyone was impeccably dressed.

Stephe and Max were the only two humans on the planet, yet were never overtly stared at. The people of Khorlu were used to seeing strange species. And oh, the species Stephe and Max saw while they were there! Tall, short, rotund, rolling, willowing, green, blue, white, gray and orange. It was a sea of "humanity"—there's a word! The very nature of the word "humanity" was about to change forever.

They got their videos and photo ops: in the Senate, on Allauch Avenue, the main drag of Khorlu—it was the Champs Elysées of the city. Allauch Avenue was was ultimately a thousand miles long, one huge road ending at the Senate Building in ChongJi. The Acropolis was the old, original seat of power in Khorlu's pre-space days, a crumbling ruin.

They went to shops; the Guelph obviously liked buying clothes. Furniture shops, "coffee" shops—or whatever stimulant it was. The store they spent the most time at was a pet store on Allauch Avenue. Not only because it was the largest on the planet, but because of the dizzying array of animals on display. Creatures that defied categorization. Puppy-dog-like things with four legs and a tail and the meltiest green eyes. Very cuddly. Also cuddly were the "cats"—not quite like Earth cats, but close. Birds and reptiles and exotic creatures that boggled the mind.

Stephe wanted to get one of the dogs, but Max talked him out of it. At least for now.

Ch'Shock was not in attendance for most of the visit, as he had pressing business matters to attend to.

Their four days were a blur. They found that transportation was a dream. Travel tubes, subways, autonomous people movers meant they could go anywhere, effortlessly.

They went to the Offworld Museum, studying the various members of the Grand Society, and all the underdeveloped worlds. They found the display for Earth—it was not flattering. Despite Ch'Shock's reassuring words back on the Moon, it was clear that not all species were allowed in, nor did all species welcome the Grand Society. A whole section of the museum was devoted to First Contacts Gone Wrong. Several species, upon first contact, got violent and kicked the Grand Society out, refusing to participate, instead falling back in on themselves and their warring ways. And others were refused admittance.

Would Earth suffer the same fate? Stephe couldn't help but wonder.

On their third day, a morning they were spending lounging naked in their hotel suite, exhausted, they'd ordered brunch. Stephe's Muon rang. Who would be calling him on Khorlu?

It was Ch'Shock. Being naked, he didn't use his camera.

"Stephe, you and Max have been invited to ChongJi, to the Integration Ministerial Building. I believe a decision has been made regarding Earth's admittance to the Grand Society. Can you be there at 11 a.m.?"

"Absolutely!" Stephe's heart was pounding.

"I've just Muoned you the location of the building; go ahead and take a taxi. We'll be expecting you at 11."

This was it. Stephe was sick. If Earth was denied entry into the Grand Society then all the suffering in the U.S. would continue indefinitely. He wanted to throw up. Even as he and Max hurried through their showers and got dressed, he was full of dread. All those people in prison, their only chance was coming today at 11 and it was completely out of his hands.

Down 148 floors, they got into a driverless taxi and, by waving his Muon over the control, Stephe set their destination in ChongJi.

They held hands in the cab, which floated on a cushion of air and glided as if by magic through the traffic of Khorlu, and up Allauch Avenue.

"Max, what are we going to do if this doesn't work?" Stephe asked, looking worried.

"I've been thinking about this." Good old Max. "If we're not allowed into the Grand Society then we're going to have to do this the old fashioned way. We'll have to resort to terrorism if need be. It could mean war, but we have to stop those states from persecuting innocent people. I'm personally ready to step up and get out of my comfort zone. We'll take them back by force. No more Mr. Nice Guy. We kinda gave up down there; I'm not willing to do that anymore."

He continued, "We'll have to start with the right to vote and end the voter fraud; I don't know what can be done, but whatever it is we'll find it."

Stephe had never heard Max so fired up before. It was wonderful.

Whatever the news, they had work to do and, by God, they *were* going to do it!

Suddenly they were there. Integration Ministerial Building. It was the half-mile high building that dominated the city skyline. It corkscrewed up like a mad creation with cantilevered tiers and gardens all the way up. The top of the building was obscured by pink clouds in the purple-blue sky.

Ch'Shock met them at the entrance. They shook hands.

"The hearing room is in the Third Quadrant," Ch'Shock said warmly. "Please come this way."

They found the elevators to the correct section of the building and zoomed up at terrific speed; Stephe's ears popped. Once at the Third Quadrant lobby, they changed to a local elevator and went to the 103rd floor.

It was as much a boulevard as it was a hallway; beings of all sorts hurried about in business attire. Ch'Shock led them to a large room like a court room or senate hearing chamber; at the dais were nine beings in robes. They were speaking various languages, *beeps, boops* and *bops*; Stephe was getting to where he could recognize the Guelph language from all the others. Their Muons translated for them:

". . . recognize the need for due haste in this matter. I'd like to once again enter into the record the following submission by Earth Human Stephen Stafford." And they played his report! Stephe felt embarrassed as a 3-D version of his ten-minute report played on the large screen. As always, Stephe registered slight shock at the sound of his own voice; he seemed more nasal than he heard himself in his head.

"The people of Earth have accomplished great things," Stephe began on the screen, standing casually in front of a backdrop of images. He'd worked hard to make it breezy, like a travel blog, and he couldn't help but feel a certain pride in his work.

"As a collection of societies, we have grown from Paleolithic times through our industrial revolution, through periods of great war and even greater peace . . ." Stephe found he was mouthing the words along with the 3-D video and grimaced at a few mistakes he'd made. The video showed early man, biblical and Chinese history, the Iron Age, the Dark Ages, the Renaissance and cathedrals, temples and art. Then he showed the wars, adding that as horrible as they were, they always ended. He heavily featured the end of World War II and the atomic blast, then Man's early forays to the Moon, culminating with our current world gone mad with climate change, jailing of innocent segments of the population, the dissolution of the United States, the superpowers of Russia, China and India. He continued:

As far as we've come, we're at an impasse. Pollution and climate change are beginning to take a heavy toll and we've only just begun our journeys into space. With the onset of personal technology, we're facing unparalleled corruption: for-profit prisons have 10 percent of the population in some areas held without charges and our democracies have fallen apart.

We believe we have a lot to offer to the Grand Society in terms of art, inventiveness, creativity and passion. We just need help getting through our growing pains.

Thank you for your attention to this proposal.

And the screen went blank. A splattering of applause—taking various forms by various species—echoed in the chamber.

The person who seemed to be the chairman on the dais spoke first. "I understand Stephe Stafford is with us today; would you please stand, Mr. Stafford?"

Stephe was horrified and nervous. He stood. Another sprinkle of applause.

"Mr. Stafford, do you truly feel your species has merit?"

"I do, Your Honor." He hoped the title "Your Honor" would be appropriately translated into the proper language and that he was considered respectful.

The leader continued: "What do you believe would happen to your world, Mr. Stafford, if membership into the Grand Society were withheld?"

"Well," Stephe replied, "I believe we'd continue to descend into pollution and corruption; that it would get far worse until society once again rose up in bloody conflict—a rebellion, another war unlike any war we've had so far. Many lives would be lost."

"And wouldn't that be a war of your own making?"

"It would. With no guarantee that it would have a favorable outcome."

Someone else on the dais spoke. "Perhaps it would be advantageous to let Earth's population kill each other and thin out the herd before First Contact."

Several seemed to agree. Stephe felt sick to his stomach at the prospect.

"Let us retire to chambers and hear from our constituents," the leader said. "We will release our decision at fourteen o'clock. Meeting adjourned."

Stephe sank back down into his chair next to Max and Ch'Shock.

"You did well, Stephe," Max said. "Your presentation was excellent."

"Thank you. How long until fourteen o'clock?"

"That's in about two hours," Ch'Shock said. "I think lunch would be in order. It will, of course, be my treat."

They went up in the building to the Fourth Quadrant—the highest section of the building—and had lunch on the roof. The view was intense. The clouds had blown away and it was like being in an airplane with unobstructed vistas. They had the caffeine-like beverage and sandwiches and salads, and then they sat talking for a while.

"I'm afraid the view that some of your species needs to die out first will be a popular one," Ch'Shock admitted. "I know it must seem very macabre to you, but there are practical considerations. Nine billion people need more resources than six billion do; if I'm any judge of history, your planet is ready for quite a population contraction. You haven't had any plagues lately; you're long overdue for one."

"I can't believe we're talking about three billion people dying," Max said, somewhat savagely.

"It's just a question of numbers, really," Ch'Shock answered. Stephe had liked Ch'Shock, until that.

"But we're talking about people!" Stephe said.

"Yes, we are," Ch'Shock agreed. "And about what's to be done with them. We're operating on a different scale now. There are forty-six billion creatures in the Grand Society. I hope another nine billion will join. In either case, we'll find out shortly. It's almost fourteen o'clock."

They went back to the courtroom and the proceedings continued.

The chairman stood and spoke: "The council has deliberated and reached a conclusion. It has been decided that the planet known as Earth shall be granted membership into the Grand Society, on Earth's calendar day July 1, 2037; that's about fifteen standard days from now. This meeting is adjourned. Thank you."

Their four days in Khorlu had come to an end. It was time to go back to Earth's Moon and get ready for First Contact.

Stephe diligently wrote in his journal all that had transpired. He kept a complete record and spent most of the four days on the ride home in the cabin he shared with Max, putting together a cohesive picture from the jumble of images in his head.

Stephe never thought he'd feel let down and bored with being on the Moon. But here it was. Dull gray rock, recycled air—after the open purple skies of Khorlu, the Moon felt like a rat's nest.

The people of Earth had no idea what was coming.

Tensions were up again between California and the U.S.; Europe was fighting and the Middle East was on the brink of collapse—since the oil money started to dry up they were in a battle amongst themselves, threatening Israel with annihilation.

Stephe's job was to present the assembled guests on Earth—he started to wonder if he'd just get shot—to prepare a video piece on Homeworld and to give the overview of what was about to happen. It was, obviously, the biggest news story of his life. But how to write it?

He edited together the videos of Homeworld first; that was easy. That was his job. But instead of bullets and lynchings and firebombings, it was shopping and a pet store and the latest fashions. He featured Max heavily in the videos, being as proud of him as he was. He was proud of the video piece; he'd become a pretty good broadcaster after all.

Chapter 25

Date of First Contact: July 1, 2037. The Guelph ship was smaller than the one upon which they travelled to Homeworld. It was metallic blue. Flight time between the moon and Earth wasn't 456 minutes in a Guelph ship; they made the trip in just twenty minutes.

Destination: New York City, New York. United Nations Plaza. It made sense. The message was for everyone on Earth, not one specific country.

The ship hovered over the lawn at United Nations Plaza and waited for an hour.

As technologically advanced as Earth had become, there was nothing in existence that could quietly hover over the grass at the United Nations as well as the beautiful Guelph ship did. It was extraordinary. They'd arranged to wait thus for one hour, no signals or communications; just hovering, fifteen yards off the ground so police and news people had a chance to gather.

Everyone had their cameras out; the news streamed live across the planet. It had everyone's attention. The police had their weapons drawn.

When the hour was up the ship settled noiselessly onto the grass.

Acknowledgments

Nanowrimo! I can't say enough. Thank you National Novel Writing Month, each November, for being there, encouraging us all to get to 50,000 words by the end of the month. Thank you to Heide Simmons next door for telling me about Nanowrimo in the first place—you have sparked something in me that, perhaps to the chagrin of my readers, will not be silenced. I'd like to thank Paul D. Cain for re-introducing me to writing at a naked pool party one day; Mark E. Anderson, my publisher, for being such a professional influence; and especially my editor Lynn Green: y'all're mean. Thank you for that.

I'd like to thank my mom, Mary Pennington for listening to me whine and for giving me encouragement, and to my BFF Deborah Kelch for always being there and rooting for me.

Finally, thank you to my boyfriend George Thomas for being the ultimate artistic inspiration. Thanks for showing me what it looks like to complete works of art and thank you for being my friend.

Did you enjoy 2037?

Pick up your copy of *Bears In The Raw* co-authored by Luke Mauerman at amazon.com.

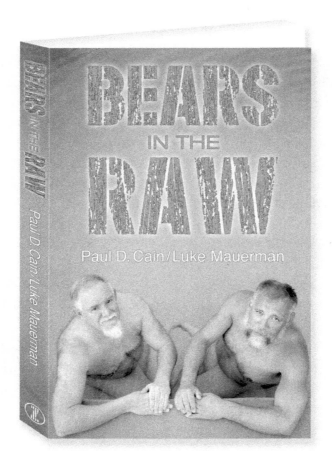

CPSIA information can be obtained
at www.ICGtesting.com
Printed in the USA
BVHW072046180220
572579BV00040B/417